Zack moved so gradually, he hardly seemed to move at all.

And then he was just inches from her. The slightest movement and they would touch.

The tiles of the pool's wall pressed against Ava's shoulder blades. She fought for breath. "It's a terrible idea," she whispered.

"Agreed. And yet, here we are."

"Something about you just drives me wild," she admitted.

His mouth curved in a devastating smile. "Hmm. I can work with that."

Suddenly, she was drifting toward him.

"It's going to be hard to put this back in the box," he warned. "Just be aware."

Ava laid her hands on Zack's shoulders. Her fingers twisted into the sodden cotton of his shirt and against the thick, hard muscles beneath. She let her legs float up to twine around his. "I don't want it in a box," she whispered as their lips touched.

* * *

Tall, Dark and Off Limits by Shannon McKenna is part of the Men of Maddox Hill series.

Dear Reader,

I go for stories where the hero and heroine have been secretly crushing on each other for years. Add the lure of the forbidden (she's his best friend's little sister, and his boss's niece, ooh la la!), stir vigorously and voilà, you've got *Tall, Dark and Off Limits*, book three of the Men of Maddox Hill series.

To Zack, Ava is the golden girl of Maddox Hill, while Zack is a self-made man. He's worked his way up to be the chief security officer at a globe-spanning architecture firm, and he's proud of his achievements. But with Ava, he feels like a tongue-tied, overgrown soldier boy.

When Ava needs help with a security problem, Zack is as stiff and forbidding as he is gorgeous, but his protective instincts kick instantly into high gear. Is it an opportunity to break down the wall between them...or a powder keg destined to explode? Neither can resist finding out.

I hope you like the final installment of Men of Maddox Hill. Check out book one, Drew Maddox and Jenna Somerses' story, *His Perfect Fake Engagement*. Then give book two, *Corner Office Secrets*, Vann Acosta and Sophie Valente's story, a try! And I've got a delicious new series in the works, so sign up for my newsletter at shannonmckenna.com for updates!

Enjoy Zack and Ava's story, and let me know what you think! I love to hear from readers.

Much love,

Shannon McKenna

SHANNON McKENNA

TALL, DARK AND OFF LIMITS

ISBN-13: 978-1-335-73539-3

Tall, Dark and Off Limits

This edition published by arrangement with Harlequin Books S.A.

For questions and comments about the quality of this book, please contact us at CustomerService@Harlequin.com.

Harlequin Enterprises ULC
22 Adelaide St. West, 41st Floor
Toronto, Ontario M5H 4E3, Canada
www.Harlequin.com

Printed in U.S.A.

Shannon McKenna is the *New York Times* and *USA TODAY* bestselling author of over twenty-five romance novels. She ranges from romantic suspense to contemporary romance to paranormal, but in all of them, she specializes in tough, sexy alpha male heroes, heroines with the brains and guts to match them, blazing sensuality, and of course, the redemptive power of true love. There's nothing she loves more than abandoning herself to the magic of a pulse-pounding story. Being able to write her own romantic stories is a dream come true.

She loves to hear from her readers. Contact her at her website, shannonmckenna.com, for a full list of her novels. Find her on Facebook at Facebook.com/authorshannonmckenna to keep up with her news. Or join her newsletter at shannonmckenna.com/connect.php and look for the juicy free book you'll get as a welcome gift! She hopes to see you there!

Books by Shannon McKenna

Men of Maddox Hill

His Perfect Fake Engagement
Corner Office Secrets
Tall, Dark and Off Limits

Visit her Author Profile page at Harlequin.com, or shannonmckenna.com, for more titles.

You can also find Shannon McKenna on Facebook, along with other Harlequin Desire authors, at Facebook.com/harlequindesireauthors!

One

"How long has this been going on?"

The fury in Zack Austin's voice rocked Ava Maddox back in her chair.

Whoa. She'd come to his office for advice from him. Insights. Ideas. Professional experience. Maybe even a little comfort and reassurance.

She had *not* come here to be scolded like a bad little kid.

"A while now." She kept her voice cool. "I've been noticing the trolls for about a year now. But it really escalated in the past few weeks. I started getting worried about it after I got back from my trip to Italy. Then the last couple of weeks, they started really swarming me. Then came the hack. So call it five weeks, give or take a couple of days."

"Five weeks." Zack's voice was savage. "Five goddamn weeks, Ava. That's how long it took you to say something to me about this."

"I'm saying something now." Ava's voice sharpened, despite her best efforts to stay calm. "It started small, you understand? In the comments section of my videos and posts. Cracks about my body, sexual stuff, 'shut up and make me a sandwich' comments. It's a shame, but professional women get used to it. I haven't been hiding anything from you. I'm just cultivating a thick skin and trying not to sweat it. As one does."

"And you let it get to this point before you said something? Seriously?"

Ava opened her mouth to let him have it, and then closed it. She inhaled. Let out a slow, relaxing breath, counting down. Five. Four. Three. Two. One. *Calm.*

Maybe coming to Zack hadn't been such a great idea after all. The chief security officer of her uncle's architecture firm, Maddox Hill, was totally beside himself. And Zack Austin was intimidating even in a good mood.

Why all this thundering intensity, for God's sake? She had not seen that coming. The general sense she got from Zack could best be described as chilly disapproval. And it had been even chillier ever since that fateful night at his apartment six years ago.

The one she could barely stand to think about without writhing in embarrassment.

Now look at him. Towering over her with those burning eyes and balled-up fists, a muscle twitching in his jaw. The exact opposite of chilly. It was almost scary.

"It started out about a year ago, on complaint sites," she told him, keeping her voice low and even. "Those are websites that let people anonymously harass anyone who pisses them off. I tried to get the posts taken down, but it's almost impossible without paying them off, and I will not give those leeches money. I've talked to the police at various times, but they made it clear that there's not much they can do, since I can't prove physical danger or monetary damages."

"They don't think this indicates physical danger?" Zack stabbed his finger at the photo, which she'd taken this morning with her cell phone.

Slut was spray-painted across her garage in big red letters. Her haters knew exactly where she lived. And they wanted her to think about that fact. All the time.

"They'll investigate, of course," Ava said. "But up until now, it's just been toxic ugliness. No crimes."

"I'll set the cybersecurity team on it immediately," Zack said. "Sophie should be back from Italy soon. I want her to make this her first priority."

"I doubt she'll have much luck," Ava said. "Whoever these people are, they're very good. I've had my computer wizard friends look into it for me, and they told me that whoever's posting always masks their IP and scrubs their metadata."

"We'll see," Zack said darkly. "We'll just see about that."

"I was trying to look on the bright side until this morning," Ava admitted. "The posts were nasty, and they're engineered for good SEO, but I have a robust online presence and lots of preexisting content, so they never floated too high in the search engine results. Then yesterday I got hacked, and my social media feeds were flooded with this crap. And this morning was the vandalism. The detective I've been in touch with suggested a security camera. Which I already have, but it hasn't been working, and I've been too busy to get it fixed. I will, of course, take care of that as soon as possible."

"You don't have a working security camera?" Zack sounded personally offended. "Good God, Ava. I'll get someone over there first thing to get a system installed."

"Please, don't worry about it. I can take care of it myself."

"You haven't been taking care of anything, from what I can see. I should have known about this from the very first rude comment that showed up. And while your brother and your uncle are away, I'm responsible for—"

"Nothing." Her voice rang out, loud enough to be heard outside his closed office door. "You are responsible for nothing, Zack. I am a grown woman. I run my own company. I have spoken to the police. They don't think I'm in danger, but they suggest that I be cautious, and I intend to follow their advice. Coming to you was just a courtesy. I wanted you in the loop. So would Drew and my uncle, I'm sure."

He flicked through the pictures and screenshots on her tablet again. "You've given all this to the police, I assume."

"Of course," she said. "I've been documenting it from the beginning."

"Jesus," he muttered. "LyingCheatingSluts. Scammerbot. NaughtyGirlsReports. It just pisses me off that these filthy scumbags can post absolutely anything they want, with no fact checking. No accountability."

"And no recourse," she said. "The sites won't respond to emails. It's a nightmare."

Zack paused over one post, one she recognized even from a distance and at an extreme angle, one of the ones posted on the She'sASkank site. A not-so-hot picture of her, in her black-rimmed nerd girl glasses, hair wildly mussed, mouth wide-open like she was yelling at someone, with a banner across her that read, *Impostor. Fraud. Skank.*

The caption on the bottom read, "This drug-addicted hooker and known sexual deviant is trying to go legit. She's passing herself off as a PR expert. Don't fall for it. She's nothing but trash. Remember...you were warned." The Gilchrist House address for Blazon PR & Branding Specialists, along with all their contact info, was included.

The whole thing was jacking up her anxiety to stratospheric heights. She would have called her brother, Drew, or her best friend, Jenna, for emotional support, but as it happened, they were off on their blissful honeymoon. She might even have confided in her moody and difficult uncle, Malcolm, but he was gone, too, off to Italy, to get to know his recently rediscovered biological daughter, Sophie Valente. Ava didn't want to upset the dynamics of that budding relationship. In fact, she'd gone to Italy herself at the beginning, just to check Sophie out for herself, and she'd concluded that Sophie was fabulous. Strong, kind, funny, smart. A cousin well worth having. So that was all good.

That said, being alone with this problem sucked. She was looking over her shoulder, and she felt nervous and vulnerable, even inside her own locked house.

So here she was with Zack, the security expert. But the look on his face made her doubt her judgment in having told him. She'd been afraid that he would think she was blowing things out of proportion. Trying to garner attention. Suddenly, out of nowhere, she was the one trying to calm him down.

"It makes me so angry, I want to kill someone," Zack said.

"Ah… I'm gratified at your concern," she said carefully. "But don't, okay? I have enough problems right now."

Zack made an irritated sound in the back of his throat and got up, turning his back to her to stare out the window at the downtown Seattle skyline, glittering in the darkness. Which gave her the always-welcome spectacle of the amazing way his white shirt fit over his big, broad, hard-muscled back. His long, strong legs. The way his dress pants hugged his taut, magnificent backside. *Wow.*

Noticing that made her pissed at herself. Because yes, in spite of his coldness, in spite of the hard, flinty look in his gray eyes, she still found the guy ridiculously hot.

He wore his hair buzzed to almost military shortness, a nod to his tours in Iraq with the marines. That was where he'd met her brother, Drew Maddox, the firm's CEO, and Vann Acosta, the CFO. A trio of overachievers, set to take over the world together—in a good way. Drew and Vann had let their hair grow back out to civilian lengths, but not Zack. He still had that tough, sexy-soldier-boy vibe going on, and it just got to her. Every time she saw the back of his muscular neck and his thick scrub brush of shiny brown hair fading to stubble on his nape and ears, she imagined how it would feel to touch it.

She'd bet it would feel both crisp and soft against her fingertips. Delicate friction.

But she'd never made any headway in charming the guy. Maybe that was why she had such an outsize crush on him. How kinky and self-defeating was that.

And the insanity of that night six years ago didn't help. She still couldn't believe she'd gone to his apartment. He'd mixed up a pitcher of margaritas, and she had pounded those until she got up the nerve to throw herself at him. Tried to kiss him.

That was as far as she remembered. She'd woken up in his bed the next morning, fully clothed, a blanket laid over her. Head splitting. He'd brewed coffee, left a bottle of Advil on the counter next to it and gone to work. No word, no note, no call. No clue.

Zack had never said a word about it. And in six long years, she still hadn't worked up the nerve to ask him what the hell had happened that night. It was anybody's guess.

No wonder he was cold. Disapproving. God knew what he must think of her.

She had tried for years to convince herself that Zack just wasn't her type. Not mentally, not emotionally, even physically. He was too damn big, for one thing. Rough features, big head, broad face, square jaw. That deep, scratchy voice, usually barking orders to someone. Pale gray eyes, sharp and electric, and narrowed to suspicious slits, or at least they were whenever she was around. A grim, sealed mouth. She had seen him smile before. Just not at her. He had a gorgeous smile.

Even so, with his crooked, bumpy nose and the diagonal white slash through one of his thick eyebrows, he looked like he should be in full body armor with an M-4 carbine slung over his shoulder. He had that rough-and-ready warrior vibe, even in a bespoke suit.

He'd made it clear that he considered her public relations and social media management for Maddox Hill to be frivolous make-work. Something to keep her busy. Her uncle was the firm's founder and her big brother was the CEO, so nepotism, right? Calling her to work as a PR consultant was just throwing the little rich girl a bone. Keeping her out of trouble.

She activated the inner mantra that she always used when dealing with Zack.

Repeat after me. You do not need to prove yourself to that man.

Yup, good thing she didn't need Zack Austin's approval to do her professional thing. And to crush it, too, for that matter.

"Which detective did you talk to at the police department?" he demanded.

"I spoke to Detective Leland MacKenzie. But there's no need for you to get involved. I can handle the police."

He turned back. "I'd rather be in the loop. If this escalates, I'll want to coordinate all possible resources to go after this filthy scum."

The violence in his voice startled her afresh. "Whoa," she said. "Don't overreact."

"That trash was right outside your house last night

as you slept. With nothing but a lock between him and you. What kind of locks do you have on your door?"

"There's only one, and I can't tell you off the top of my head, but it looks big and substantial," she assured him. "I'll text you a picture of it when I get home."

"You aren't going home," he said. "Not alone, anyway. That's out of the question. You can't be anywhere alone until this bastard is pulped."

Ava held up her hands. "Zack, take a deep breath."

"Do not jerk me around. I know that's your specialty, but not today."

Ava shot to her feet, stung. "My specialty? Where the hell did that come from? When have I jerked you around?"

"I'm sorry. That came out wrong. But this is dead serious, and I can't let you—"

"I know! But I'm better off handling it on my own than watching you freak out about it! Excuse me, Zack. I'm out of here."

Zack stepped between her and the exit, blocking her. "Wait."

"No." She glared up at him. Damn, the man was tall. "Get the hell out of my way, and I'll get the hell out of yours. Now would be good. Scoot over, please."

"Ava." His voice was quieter now. "No."

The sound of her name, spoken by that deep, rough voice, made her shiver. And that pissed her off even more. "It's not up to you," she snapped. "Don't force me to make a scene. It would be embarrassing for us both." She fixed him with her best sudden-death glare. "I swear, I will screech like a banshee."

Zack didn't budge. "I shouldn't have said that. It was unfair."

She let out a sharp laugh. "Ya think?"

"I apologize," he said gruffly. "It just… This situation really got under my skin."

She swallowed. "Mine, too," she admitted.

"Please," he urged. "Sit down. Please, let's talk about this like normal people."

She realized, after her butt hit the chair, that the guy had herded her smoothly right back into her seat, using she knew not what tricks of mind magic and charisma.

She clutched the arms of the chair. "I should go now."

"Please understand, I can't just let this be," Zack told her. "I might not be responsible for your choices or your behavior, but as CSO of Maddox Hill, I am responsible for your safety, and I take that responsibility seriously."

He was casting a spell on her. Those intense eyes. This close, she could see his beard shadow. If she touched the stark angles of his jaw and ran her fingers against the grain, she'd feel that fine, sandpaper rasp. Supple and hot. She had to stop this. Right now.

"Zack," she said. "It's been a long day, so be clear. Are you apologizing to me or bullying me? Because you can't seem to make up your mind."

That actually got a smile out of him, because miracles did happen. It was brief and fleeting, but she saw it, and it involved amazing dimples. Long, deep-carved dimples that accented the gorgeous lines that bracketed his mouth.

"I'm apologizing," he said. "And I'm laying down the law. Respectfully."

She snorted. "I didn't know law could be laid down

respectfully. I believe that's usually done by force. Which I'm not in the mood for, if you haven't noticed."

He studied her thoughtfully, like he was pondering how best to manage her.

Her heart thudded. Because he'd smiled. Because of all this intense interest he was displaying. She was reacting to him exactly like the kind of silly, attention-hungry bubblehead he already thought she was.

Pull yourself together, girl. Stay tough.

It took all her nerve, but she manufactured a cool, remote smile and twitched the tablet back. "I'll just take that, thanks." She closed the files, slipped the tablet into her briefcase and stood. "Lay down all the laws you want. I'll get on with my day. 'Bye."

He glanced at his watch. "It's eight forty p.m. You have more day to get through?"

She shrugged. "That's nobody's business but mine."

"At the risk of being rude, it's my business now. And your agenda for the evening just changed."

She blinked at him. "Did it? Good to know."

He ignored that. "Tonight, we're going through your life with a microscope and tweezers. I want to know everyone who could be angry at you. Disgruntled employees, professional rivals, ex-boyfriends, jealous girlfriends of ex-boyfriends, rejected would-be boyfriends—the sky's the limit. Anyone who might hold a grudge. Whatever you had planned for the evening, it's off. You're not leaving my sight until we fix this."

Ava was astonished. "I beg your pardon?"

"You heard me." His eyes were like points of bright, cold steel.

She tried to breathe, but the air wouldn't go in. She

had not anticipated this intense, intractable, incredibly difficult version of Zack Austin.

"Let me get this straight," she said. "You want a comprehensive list of everyone who might disapprove of me before bedtime? That's not happening."

"You piss people off that much?"

"Yes, I do," she said. "Blazon does all kinds of different work, and some of my projects are controversial. I try to make them go viral, and often I succeed. Eliciting strong emotions is my stock-in-trade. It's an unfortunate law of nature that any time you try to change anything big, someone will get upset about it. Particularly if you're a woman."

Zack looked puzzled. "Change what? I thought your job was to boost Maddox Hill's search engine optimization and raise our profile on the social media platforms. What's controversial about that?"

Oh, God, where to even begin. "Maddox Hill is just a small slice out of the pie chart of my professional activity, Zack," she explained patiently. "I'm a consultant. Blazon has many different clients. Maddox Hill is only one of them."

"Ah," he said. "I did not know that."

"You learn something new every day," she said. "If you pay attention."

His eyes were locked with hers. The seconds ticked by. She held the connection.

"I'm paying attention now." He sat down at his desk and folded his arms, leaning toward her. "Tell me about the rest of the pie. Slice by slice. Go back as far as you can remember."

"We'd be here until tomorrow morning, and we'd

have only just begun," Ava warned him. "I've got a lot of stuff happening. Blazon is a boutique branding and marketing company, so every project is different. We tell stories about products or services, in whatever manner or on whatever platform resonates with the target audience. We also design trade show exhibits. An offshoot of a job I had a few years ago. I'm still partnered with the people who produce and deliver the physical booths. But my real love is making the videos. That's what I enjoy the most, and what I want to focus on."

"Like the videos you made for Jenna, for Arm's Reach?"

Ava was startled that he knew about those videos. She'd made them to help her best friend and now sister-in-law, Jenna, an engineer who designed cutting-edge prosthetic arms. "Exactly. They're becoming more like documentary films. I'm thinking of hiring more staff so that I can concentrate on that. When this troll problem is solved, of course."

"How many of these video projects have you done?"

She shrugged, trying to count. "I don't know," she said. "At least six or seven the past year or so. Maybe fifteen more in the three years before that."

He tapped his fingers against the desk, considering options. "We're going to need to get some dinner," he said. "Shall I order in, or do you want to go out?"

Ava realized something all at once. She'd had that sour, heavy feeling inside her for so long now. Whatever else she might be doing during the course of her day, she was also simultaneously worrying about her online haters and their toxic hostility. The anger, frustration, intimidation…it was like a cold rock inside her. Weighing her down.

But since she'd been in this room with Zack, she hadn't felt that cold weight inside. Not even a little bit. She'd had all the feels, for sure. But not that one.

And this dizzy, dangerous buzz was way more fun.

That did not, however, mean she had the nerve to hang out with Zack Austin in the Maddox Hill building all night, in his office, with darkness and silence all around.

"Let's go out," she said. "We can talk at the restaurant."

"Fine. Do you have any preferences? Italian, steakhouse, barbecue, sushi, fusion?"

"Anything is fine," she said. "Surprise me."

He hit his intercom. "Amelia? Are you still there?"

"Just heading out," his administrative assistant said through the speaker.

"Before you go, could you make a last-minute dinner reservation for two? Nearby. Something quiet, preferably with booths. We're ready to go now."

"I'll see what I can do," Amelia told him.

"Thanks." He put the phone down and met her gaze again. "So? Make the call."

"What call?" she asked.

His brows came together. "To cancel your evening plans."

She almost laughed. Her evening plans had involved going back to the Blazon office at Gilchrist House to take care of some final paperwork for the trade show and calling a car to take her home. Then maybe some yogurt and a piece of fruit, and she'd at least try to get some sleep. She probably wouldn't succeed, but hope sprang eternal.

And Zack thought she was going out clubbing in a sequined gown. Wild thing.

She'd almost prefer he keep thinking that, but she didn't have the energy to lie.

"No plans," she admitted.

His eyes narrowed for a moment before he spoke. "Good."

The rough satisfaction in that single word felt like a physical touch. It set off a million tiny fireworks inside her. Fizzy excitement, keeping bad feelings at bay.

Damn. It was just body chemistry. A cheap trick. Endorphins buzzing through her body. It was an absolutely terrible idea. She'd end up feeling worse before she was done.

But in Zack's current bulldog mood, she couldn't shake him off anyhow. So what the hell?

She might as well indulge.

Two

"No wine," Zack told the waiter brusquely, realizing too late how stuffy and uptight that sounded. "For me, of course," he said to Ava. "Feel free to have some. I never drink when I'm working."

"Good for you." She smiled up at the waiter, whose name was Martin, according to the tag on his shirt. "I'll have a glass of red wine, please."

"I have a beautiful 2016 Romanée-Conti that's open," Martin told her.

"Sounds lovely." She gave the waiter that trademarked blinding smile that brought men to their knees. Martin stumbled off, probably to walk into walls and tables.

And Zack just sat there, tongue-tied. When Ava Maddox was around, his foot always ended up stuck so far into his mouth, he needed surgical intervention to get it out. She was giving him that look. Big, sharp blue eyes that missed nothing. So on to him.

The restaurant had low light and a hushed ambience, and they were in the back, tucked in a wood-paneled corner booth. Now the challenge was to kick-start his brain into operation, instead of just staring at how beautiful she was in the flickering candlelight.

She just waited, patiently. Like she was all too used to men losing their train of thought as soon as they made eye contact with her. Like she was accustomed to cutting the poor stammering chumps some slack while they pulled themselves together.

Her cell rang, and she gave him an apologetic glance when she saw the display. "Gotta take this. One sec." She tapped the screen and held it to her ear. "Ernest? Thanks for getting back to me. Are you still in the office?… Yeah? Could you get a cab to swing by the Mathesson Pub and Grill on your way home?… Yeah, I need my laptop, the pink one with the collage cover. I'm talking to the Maddox Hill CSO about the online harassment…yeah, I know, but still…uh-huh. Okay, thanks. You're my hero. Later, then."

She laid the phone down. "Ernest is my assistant. He'll bring my computer here so I can show you the master list of the last few of years' worth of Blazon's projects."

"I'm surprised you don't have your laptop with you at all times," he said.

"I usually do," she said. "But I had every intention of going back to Gilchrist House tonight. I have a crazy weekend coming up. Ernest and I are flying down to the Future Innovation trade show in Los Angeles tomorrow. It's a very big deal."

Zack couldn't hide his disapproval. "Traveling to Los Angeles? Going back to a deserted office late in the evening? Leaving by yourself, going home by yourself? With all this going on?"

Ava sighed. "Zack, Gilchrist House has a twenty-four-hour doorman. And I would call a car to take me from doorstep to doorstep. I'm not an idiot."

"I never suggested that you were."

"I'm not in physical danger," Ava assured him. "Really. This is just, you know, the new normal. The incivility of our modern electronic age. It's ugly and unsavory, but I've got to get used to it and learn to roll with it."

"The hell you do," he said. "New normal, my ass. I'll tell you what's normal. When I find that bottom-feeding son of a bitch and grind him into paste."

Ava gave him that narrow, nervous look, which by now he recognized. It was a signal that he wasn't behaving professionally. He was too intense. Making it personal.

In a word, scaring her.

"Ah, wow, Zack," she murmured. "I'm surprised at your reaction."

"Why? This situation is a disgrace. Why should you be surprised that I'm horrified?"

Her eyes slid away. "Well, I don't know. It's just that you've never taken me seriously before, so why would you suddenly take me seriously now?"

"I'm sorry I gave you that impression," he said stiffly. "It wasn't intentional."

"Oh, don't be that way." Her tone was light. "I'm

used to it. I rub a lot of people the wrong way. I'm just too much for people sometimes. Drew's always on my case about it, telling me to tone it down. And I try, I really do. But it never works. Boom, out it comes. The real Ava, right in your face."

"He shouldn't do that," Zack said forcefully.

"Shouldn't what? Sorry, but I'm not following you."

"Drew. He shouldn't be on your case. He shouldn't tell you to tone it down."

Her eyes were big. "Ah… I didn't mean to get you all wound up."

"You're goddamn right, I'm wound up. I'm freaking furious, Ava. That sewer-rat troll who's bothering you? He doesn't have the right to even look at you. Let alone throw his filth at you. It pisses me off to see a lady treated that way. You don't deserve it."

She laughed under her breath. "Lady, hmm? That's sweet, but I'm sure Uncle Malcolm would have something pointed to say about that characterization of me."

"Malcolm can say anything he wants," Zack retorted. "I mean it like my mom used to mean it. It has nothing to do with manners or clothes or social status or that crap. A lady is any woman who commands respect as her due. That means you. Absolutely."

Ava appeared, for once in her life, at a loss for words. She turned away, letting her hair swing forward. A silent moment passed, and it wasn't until she pulled a tissue out of her purse that he realized, to his horror, that she was crying.

"Oh, God," he said. "Was it something I said?"

"Yes, actually," she said, blowing her nose. "That was a really great thing to hear right now, Zack. After all that nasty filth that's been coming at me. So thank you for that."

"Ah, you're welcome," he said, helplessly bemused. "You sure you're okay?"

She tossed her hair back and gave him a reassuring smile. Her long black eyelashes were wet with tears all the way around those gorgeous, mascara-smudged eyes.

"I hadn't let myself feel how much the trolling bothered me," she said, wiping the smudges away. "Even though it's stupid and insignificant, it made me feel stained. Then you said just exactly the right thing. It made me feel better. Cleaner."

Huh. Talk about a lucky freak accident. Saying just exactly the right thing to make a hot, classy, fascinating woman feel better? That was something he'd never been accused of before. But whatever. He'd take it and run with it.

"I shouldn't let myself get upset," Ava went on. "It comes with the territory."

"What? Online harassment, you mean?"

"Making enemies, in general," she said. "If you try to make a difference, you're going to make a few. It's a mathematical certainty. And I like it when people like me. I really try to be everyone's friend. I try to be thick-skinned, but this time it got to me."

"So this has happened before?" He was freshly horrified.

She smiled at him, sniffling into her tissue. "On a much smaller scale," she said. "It's never been quite this bad. It started about four years ago, while I was working on the Colby Hoyt thing."

"Name sounds familiar," he said.

"It got a lot of press. He got pushed down the stairs and broke his back. He accused his girlfriend, Judy Whelan, of pushing him, and she ended up in prison for assault, but no one knew the truth, because she had brain damage that impaired her memory, inflicted by Colby himself. His lawyers flattened Judy's public defender, and it all went to hell. But one of Judy's girlfriends was a college roommate of mine, and came to me to help get the word out. We got it all over the internet. Public interest spiked, the case was reopened and, long story short, Judy's free and Colby's in for fifteen to twenty. And a bunch of angry trolls on anonymous message boards thought that Colby was really hard done by. They like to tell me how they feel. Often, and in very strong, descriptive terms."

"I remember Hoyt," Zack said. "Spooky guy. White eyebrows and lashes."

"Yeah, that was him. That was when the trolling began in my comments sections. Then, about a year ago, Colby was up for parole, and Judy's friends and protectors were having none of that. So we pushed the video again, and his parole was denied. That was when the posts on the complaint sites started to show up. I wonder if it's connected."

"I'll be sure to look into it," Zack said as the waiter reappeared.

The guy ogled Ava's chest as he presented several plates in front of them, directing his highest-wattage smile at Ava. "Here's a sampling of our appetizers for the day. Bacon-wrapped asparagus tips deep-fried in beer batter, portobello mushrooms with three-cheese stuffing and pan-fried sage and butternut squash dumplings."

Ava stared at the tempting array of finger food, startled. “Ah, wow,” she said blankly. “Are these for someone else? I don’t think we ordered—”

“On the house,” Martin assured her. “Our treat.”

“Why, thank you,” Ava said graciously. “That’s so lovely. They look delicious.”

Zack followed Martin’s retreat with unfriendly eyes. “Does that happen a lot?”

“You mean free food, raining down from the sky?” Ava shrugged airily and popped a squash dumpling into her mouth. “Sometimes. It happens. These are really good. Try one before I eat them all.”

The disgruntled sound that came out of him made her hide a smile behind the napkin she was using to dab at her mouth. So he was entertaining her. Like a vaudeville act.

This was so tricky. He had been walking this tightrope for years. Ever since he met her, back when she was barely more than dewy-eyed jailbait. His best friend’s little sister, always there at the parties and the holidays and the barbecues. The perfect little golden-haired princess, stealing the show.

She just seemed like a different type of creature to him. Born rich, and he hadn’t been, but it was more than just that. It was like the fairies had flocked to her christening, like in that old Disney cartoon, and loaded her up with gifts. She was smart, classy, talented, well-spoken, funny. She had a gorgeous body. She sparkled; she shone. Waiters brought her unsolicited bacon-wrapped batter-fried asparagus tips, for God’s sake.

And she was so damn beautiful, he had to struggle to keep his jaw off the floor. He’d found himself catching flies more than once. Gawking at her, like the overgrown West Virginia farm boy that he was inside, in spite of the fancy suit and the corporate title. So intensely aware of his big, crooked nose, broken in a bar fight. The knife scar through his eyebrow. Souvenirs of when he was a runt getting his ass kicked. To say nothing of the battle scars from Iraq. Not that she'd judge him for that, of course. Drew had scars, too. But it was just one more thing that set her apart from him. Worlds apart.

She always seemed defensive with him. Maybe it was that night six years ago, when she'd gotten drunk at his place and then cried herself to sleep in his arms.

He still thought of those hours he'd spent, just gazing at her sleeping face.

She was probably embarrassed. Angry at herself for the lapse in judgment.

And he needed to focus on something external, something that wasn't Ava herself. He pulled his notepad out of his bag. "Let's get started. I want you to list all the—"

"Ava! There you are, hiding in the back!" It was a young, skinny guy with white-blond hair and perfectly round glasses that gave him an owl-like, steampunk appearance. Had to be Ernest, the assistant.

Ernest placed a shiny pink laptop that was covered with a laminate mosaic of photos on the table and leaned over to sniff the appetizers. "Mmm, those look great."

"Go ahead and try one," Ava suggested. "They're delicious."

Ernest popped a fried asparagus tip into his mouth

and sighed with delight as he chewed it. "Oh boy. I think I need a whole plate of these. It's a cholesterol bonanza."

"Do it, with my compliments. Put it on my card," Ava offered. "Least I can do."

"Ooh! Thanks! I will!" Ernest tried a dumpling. "Wow, yum. So, am I swinging by your place at six thirty?"

"For what? Going where?" Zack asked.

Ernest turned to him. "The airport," he said. "We're flying down to LA for the Future Innovation Trade Fair. The Bloom brothers have been nominated for the grand prize for their new soil inoculation antidesertification process. Half a million bucks. It would be a total kick in the butt if they won."

"Let's do seven a.m.," Ava said.

"No," Zack said. He turned to Ernest. "Never mind the pickup. I'll bring her directly to the airport, and we'll meet you there."

Ava's face was bewildered. "Excuse me? You'll do *what*?"

"You're not staying in your house alone tonight," he informed her. "It's not safe."

"Oh, really? Where will you be?" Ernest's eyes lit up with speculative curiosity.

"We're still working that out," Zack said.

"*I'm* working it out, Zack," she said crisply. "Last I checked, I was still making all these decisions for myself."

"You tell him, Av! Rawr!" Ernest's eyes zipped back and forth between them.

Ava made a frustrated sound and flapped her hand

at him. "Go order your food, Ernest. I'll call you in the morning and let you know what's going on."

"Will do."

But Ernest just stood there expectantly. The sparkle in his eye annoyed Zack. This was not a cage fight for this bozo's entertainment. "Good night," Zack said pointedly.

Ernest looked crestfallen. "See you in the morning!" He waggled his eyebrows at Ava. "Have fun!"

Ava put her fingers to her temples once he was gone. "Damn," she said sourly. "That I did not need, Zack."

"You still think it's okay to just run around like everything's normal?" Zack asked. "Working late, coming home late, sleeping alone, flying all over the country—"

"This is my work!" she shot back. "I will not let some mouth-breathing troll knock me off my stride! And with all due respect, I won't let you knock me off it, either!"

"So I'm in the same category as the mouth-breathing trolls?"

She rolled her eyes. "Stop it. You know perfectly well I didn't mean that. But I will continue to conduct my life exactly the way I want to. And I don't appreciate—" She cut herself off as the waiter approached.

"The rib eye for you, sir, and the pistachio-crusted salmon for you!" Martin placed the entrées in front of them with a flourish.

Zack waited until the waiter was gone before he went on. "You'll have a bodyguard 24-7 until I get to the bottom of this. But I can't pull that out of thin air at such short notice, so tonight and tomorrow, you're stuck with me. Give me the flight info so I can pass it on to Amelia. She needs to book me on your flight ASAP."

"Stuck with you? You want to fly down to LA with me? For real?"

"In normal times, the obvious solution would be for you to stay with your uncle out on Vashon Island," Zack said. "He's got good staff and a very good security system. But he's not here, and neither are Jenna or Drew. So I'm stepping up."

Zack suddenly realized that he had no clue if Ava might have a boyfriend who would not welcome his nighttime presence in her house. "Unless, ah…unless you have some other, uh, friend," he said stiffly. "That could come to stay with you. Overnight."

"No, I don't want to burden any of my friends with this," she said. "Other than you, of course. I was afraid of looking like a whiner and a wuss."

"You are neither," he told her. "On the contrary. So? Your place or mine?"

He instantly regretted the words. They sounded too suggestive. Fortunately, Ava didn't react. She was busy shaking her head back and forth like she couldn't stop herself.

"Zack, no. I'm going home. To my life. Besides, you're Maddox Hill's chief security officer. You're a busy guy with a complicated job, and you do not have time to do close protection work for me."

"I can make that call for myself," Zack said.

"I appreciate your zeal, I really do. We'll have a meeting after I get back from Los Angeles, and we'll get to work on my list then. Deal?"

"You are not staying alone tonight. End of story."

"You're not getting it." Ava shook her head, frustrated. "It's not up to you."

"I cover you until I have your security people in place, or I'll be forced to call Drew right now and tell him the situation," Zack told her. "He's in, let's see, is it Bali? I can't even remember. Then I'll call Malcolm in Italy and tell him, too. I don't know the time differences off the top of my head, and I really don't care. This is an emergency."

Ava's mouth dropped in outrage. "No way," she said. "You wouldn't."

"Oh, yeah." Zack brought out his phone and pulled Drew's number up onto the display. He let his finger hover over Call. "Your decision," he told her.

"But you can't! They'll freak out and come rushing home!"

"Rightly so," he said. "I would. If it was my sister, or my niece. In a heartbeat."

"But this is Drew's honeymoon!" she said. "And Malcolm's finally getting to know Sophie. It's important! I don't want to interrupt that!"

"Yeah, it would be a big shame," he agreed.

"You're jerking me around," she said.

"Maybe. But I'll let your family weigh in, if that's what it takes to keep you safe. We're all in this together."

Ava looked outraged, but that was just too bad. Her safety was more important than her approval.

The deathly silence stretched on and on. Ava grimly tucked away her salmon and salad, ignoring his existence. He kept himself busy with his steak.

That was only good for a few minutes, though. When the busboy whisked away their plates, there was nothing to focus on but the conversation she refused to have.

Martin reappeared, this time bearing a long, oblong

platter with several bite-size portions of various desserts. “I thought you might like a sampling of our dessert menu,” he told Ava. “Chocolate rum soufflé, apple tart with brandy sauce, key lime pie with shortbread crust, salted-caramel custard brownie cake and panna cotta with berries.”

“Oh, boy,” she murmured. “Martin, you are a very bad boy.”

“I do try.” Martin fluttered his lashes modestly. “Enjoy.”

When Martin was gone, Ava took the dessert fork and delicately scooped up a bite of the salted-caramel custard brownie. She closed her eyes as she savored it.

His lower body tightened up in response. Her eyes fluttered open, and she smiled at him. Those bright, mysterious eyes, taunting him. Owning him.

“Well?” she said. “You’re not leaving me alone with this temptation, are you?”

“Martin didn’t bring those sweets out here for me,” he said.

“We’re in this together. Isn’t that what you said?” She nudged the tray his way, then stabbed a square of caramel brownie cake and held it out. “It takes energy to shove people around. It’s going to be a long night, buddy. Do some carb-loading.”

He blew out a sigh of frustration. “Goddamn it, Ava.”

Her lips curved in a smile that made his heart speed up. “Come on, tough guy,” she murmured. “Better take your medicine. You’re going to need it.”

Three

Ava's hands shook as she shoved her things into her travel case.

Damn. What was wrong with this picture? So many things, she couldn't keep them all straight. She should not let Zack win so easily. His administrative assistant had already booked him a flight to LA tomorrow, with her and Ernest. He'd booked a room at the hotel where they were staying. There was no way to stop him from climbing all over her life.

And he had the advantage, holding the threat of calling Uncle Malcolm and her brother over her. While she was at a huge disadvantage, still not knowing what the hell had really happened on the night of the margaritas.

It made her feel so embarrassed. On top of being shaky and fluttery after that intense, sexually charged dinner date. To say nothing of weeks of worrying about vicious trolls trashing her professional reputation. She was a mess.

Zack's expression tended toward grim at the best of times, but his face had gone thunderous when she showed him the ugly graffiti spray-painted on the garage door.

Of course, a compulsory lecture followed about the complete inadequacy of her door locks and her lack of an alarm system. No surprises there. He'd also called his security staff and set a team to come and remedy that the following day. He'd called another team to work on analyzing her online harassment problem, and still a third one to set up a team of close protection agents to follow her around everywhere she went. *Yikes.*

Zack took pictures of all of it with his phone, sent them to his teams and then insisted on taking her house keys from her hand to go into her house first. He insisted on preceding her into every room.

Now, as she packed her bags, Zack was waiting out there in her living room. Probably wandering around, cataloging all the other security breaches in her house. While she stood here with her hand in her lingerie drawer, pulling out sexy, silky nighties and little bits of things with spaghetti straps and lace.

Oh, hell no. Ava whipped her hand out of that drawer as if the garments had burned her and went rummaging into the bag she'd stuffed in the closet, the one she meant to take down to the charity clothing drive. In the bottom of that bag was a set of thick fleece pajamas in hideous red plaid. It was two sizes too big and had been a Secret Santa gag gift from one of her friends. She practically swam in the thing.

Those were the pajamas for Zack Austin's house. They projected a loud, blaring signal: *Don't even think about sex. Because I'm not thinking about it. Nope, not me.*

Somehow, she got her stuff for tonight into the travel bag, and the clothes she was wearing tomorrow to the airport. Thank God she'd already packed for the trip to Los Angeles, because she would have bungled that completely in her addled state.

She gathered up the last-minute electronic bits and pieces that had to go—phone, tablet, laptop, chargers. Toiletries for tonight, since a guy with a buzz cut wasn't likely to have hair-care stuff. She took some clips and pins and scrunchies, to cover any possible hair whims for tomorrow. Then she started out into the living room, and just stopped.

Trying to slow down the frantic gallop of her heart. Calm. Collected. Adult.

She walked in to find Zack standing at the fireplace, holding her mother's high school graduation portrait in his hands. He lifted the photo, turning to her. "Your mom?"

"Yes, that's her."

He set it down carefully. "You look exactly like her." He bent to peer more closely at Mom and Dad's wedding photo. "And Drew looks just like your dad."

"So they tell me," she said, rolling her travel bag and suitcase into the living room. "It's hard for me to see. Have you finished compiling the list of all my security fails?"

"Don't be so defensive, but yes, pretty much." He sounded faintly amused. "We'll leave a set of your keys at my house for pickup, and tomorrow a team will come in here to solve them all."

"I could handle this myself, you know," she told him.

Zack gave her a level look. "Ava, this is what I do. Just let me do it."

She shrugged. "Fine, I guess. I appreciate the thought. But you're overdoing it."

"Not at all." He looked up at her Chihuly glass vase, perched on a high shelf on her bookcase. "This place really looks like you."

"What does that means? Aside from the poor security, of course."

Zack looked trapped. "I don't really know what I meant, so I shouldn't have said it in the first place. I guess, colorful, eclectic, creative, chaotic?"

"Chaotic, huh? Cluttered, you mean. That's what Uncle Malcolm says."

Zack slanted her an ironic look. "I'm not criticizing you. Not in the least. I wish you wouldn't fight me about this."

"I'm in the habit, I suppose," she said. "I fight Uncle Malcolm and Drew all the time. I can't afford to back down for one second or those two would just roll over me like a tank. So I've got this knee-jerk defensive reaction going. I know it's a pain in the butt."

"You could try just trusting me," he suggested. "I promise. It's not a trap."

She thought about that night six years ago. That morning hangover in his downtown apartment when she woke and found him gone.

The confusion and shame. The agonized curiosity.

And yet, at the restaurant, he'd called her a lady. Deserving of respect. Huh.

"My house is more secure than yours," Zack said. "That's the only reason I wanted to drag you out there tonight. I would have stayed here, if you preferred to be in your own space, but I need to pack for the trip to LA, so there's that. Maybe I am overdoing it, and I'm sorry to inconvenience you. But I will not leave you unprotected. I just can't do it."

Ava was disarmed by the intensity in his voice. "It's okay," she said. "I'm packed up for tomorrow already. I guess your place makes more sense."

He gave a brief, fleeting smile and grabbed her bags to haul them out to his car.

She tried to analyze the conflicting emotions inside her, all fighting for airtime, as she followed him out. It was nice that he cared. Nice to feel safe. No doubt about it.

But giving him his way like this…it set a bad precedent. But a precedent for what?

Her mind was running down some very dangerous paths.

When Zack was a kid, his granddad had been a local expert at breaking horses to ride. Granddad was famous in the area for his technique, the main ingredient of which was patience. He'd taught Zack his secrets, which mostly consisted of being able to let go of his own agenda and adjust completely to the animal's wavelength. To be prepared for hours to pass just waiting. Force had no part in the process. Attunement was everything.

God knew, Ava Maddox was no horse. She was proud, touchy, high-strung. But if he tried to manipulate her with force, he was going to get hammered. Eventually she was going to get sick of him holding her brother's and uncle's interference over her. She'd tell him to piss off and do his worst. At which point he wouldn't be able to protect her at all.

Patience was the only way. But having patience presupposed confidence.

With Ava, he was anything but.

The drive to his house was very quiet, giving him plenty of time to second-guess himself and quietly freak out about things he couldn't control or change. Now that he'd seen her house, he could imagine what she'd think of his own. Her place was an explosion of color and images. Provocative works of art hung on the wall, and she probably had strong, smart, articulate opinions about every one of them. Corkboards with mosaics of photos, drawings, brochures, maps, Post-it notes, quotes. Wood carvings, wind chimes. Colorful rugs and jewel-toned accent walls. Her quirky chairs and couches were upholstered with antiqued colored velvet and strewn with big puffy pillows in contrasting prints. Her outsize creative personality blazed from her living space like heat from a bonfire.

Ava Maddox didn't need an interior designer to decorate her space. It came from directly inside her head. He could wander around for hours, staring at the all the bits of stuff that interested and intrigued her. Wondering what she saw in it, and why.

His own house, large and comfortable though it was, was going to look as bland and dull as an unadorned shoebox to someone like her. He didn't have a zillion little conversation-starting windows into his soul to show off when she walked into it.

Nor was it like him to give a damn what people thought of his home. It was comfortable; it suited him. If it was good enough for him, it was good enough for anyone.

But this was Ava. Nothing could be taken for granted where she was concerned.

The gate to his driveway ground open. He drove up and parked in front of his house. They sat there in acutely uncomfortable silence for a moment.

Zack was the first to move, but Ava was out of the car before he had the chance to open her door for her. He took her suitcase and garment bag from the trunk. "This way."

She smiled in silent amusement as he unlocked the three different locks on the door, pushed it open and punched a code to disarm the alarm. "Wow. Secure."

"It's who I am," he said, flipping the lights on.

Ava walked in and looked around. The foyer with the thirty-foot-high solarium window and the slanted skylights was surrounded by a huge open-plan space, kitchen and dining room on one side and the sunken living room and big fireplace on the other. Huge windows lined both rooms. The living room had French doors leading out to a big flagstone patio. There were high ceilings with dark-stained wooden beams, a beige Berber rug. Big, long, soft couches that could handle his size, upholstered in plain, dark colors that didn't show dirt. Simple, plain table lamps. The main decoration for his living space was the view and the greenery outside, but that didn't register at night. His walls were mostly blank. No paintings or sculptures other than his gallery of family photos.

That was Zack Austin. Plain and utilitarian. What you see is what you get.

"Wow," she said. "Big."

"Yeah, I like my space." Growing up in a single-wide trailer would do that to a guy, especially a freakishly tall one. His head was probably still dented from all the ceilings and door frames he'd bashed it on.

She went down the steps into his living room, and Zack followed her down.

"I'll light a fire," he said.

"Please don't go to any trouble," she told him.

"No trouble at all. I make sure that a fire is always ready to light when I want one."

He knelt down, struck a match and touched it to the crumpled newspaper and wood shavings that lay under the little cone of kindling wood. Another of Granddad's tricks.

"You're right," she said as it blazed to life, crackling. "That was quick."

She moved closer to the fire, holding out her hands.

"Give me your jacket," he said. "I'll put it in the closet."

Ava shrugged off her jacket, releasing a soft, warm whiff of her incredible perfume. When he returned from the closet, she had wrapped her bright, patterned scarf around herself like a shawl and was studying his photo gallery.

"Your family, I take it," she said.

"Yeah, these are my nieces and nephew," he said,

pointing. "That's Bree—she's eight. And Brody, who's almost seven. And that's little Brett. She's three. That's my younger sister, Joanna, with her husband, Rick." He pointed at another photo. "That's my mom. And that's Granddad. He passed away when I was nineteen."

She smiled at the pictures. "Your nieces and nephew are gorgeous," she said. "Do they live nearby?"

"No. I wish. They're in West Virginia. Mom's not too far from my sister. She likes being close to her grandkids. I get back to see them as often as I can."

Ava studied the entire wall and looked back at him. "What about your dad?"

"He took off not long after Joanna was born," he said. "I was about three. I barely remember him."

She had a thoughtful line between her brows. "You never looked for him?"

Zack shook his head. "I figure if someone's going that far out of his way to avoid me, I should just let him. We wouldn't have much to say to each other. Are you thinking about Sophie and Malcolm, finding each other after all these years?"

"I guess I am."

"I thought about it, too. But that's different. Malcolm didn't know Sophie even existed. My dad knew all about me. He knew where we lived. He knew my mom needed money and help to raise us. He knew all that, and he didn't step up. So fuck him."

Ava nodded. "Fair enough."

He felt suddenly awkward. "Sorry. Didn't mean to get all heavy and negative."

"You weren't," she said. "Just honest. Which I like."

Those words made his body react, which was ridiculous. It was an innocent comment, and here he was, breaking out in a sweat. Imagining how it would feel to find out more things that she liked. Everything that she liked.

Every sweet, sexy, dirty detail.

He dragged his mind back on track by sheer force of will. "I was lucky. I had Granddad. My mom's father. He more than made up for the shortfall."

Ava was moving down the wall, peering closer at another photo of Granddad.

"I bet you took that photo yourself," she said.

Zack glanced at it. "Yeah, I did. That wasn't too long before he died. I was home from Iraq on leave. How did you know I took that shot?"

"The look on his face," she said softly. "The way he smiles at you. Like he's so proud. I remember that look on my parents' faces." Her voice caught.

Damn. Now his own eyes were getting all hot and prickly. No way. Not now. He was on shaky ground as it was. He groped for the first comment that came to mind. "How about Malcolm?" he asked. "Isn't he like a surrogate dad for you and Drew?"

She let out a stifled laugh. "I suppose he is. And I know he cares about me, but I have certainly never gotten that look from him."

Yikes. That was a can of worms. Thank God for the fire. The perfect distraction. He turned away swiftly to poke at the flames and lay a couple chunks of wood onto it.

Ava spoke behind him, still looking at the photo gallery. "When I first walked in, my sense was that your decorating scheme was a little impersonal. But that's not true. Looking closer at these photos, I see that it couldn't possibly be any more personal."

Zack was careful not to look up into her eyes. "I'm not much for decorating," he said. "And to be honest, I don't really have much to say about most of the art I come across. After all these years at Maddox Hill, I can talk intelligently about architecture, but not art. But photos of my family? Those I know are beautiful. No one has to tell me."

"Yes," she said. "That's exactly what I meant."

He was getting self-conscious. "How about I show you to your room and get you some fresh bedding? Then after, you can come have a nightcap by the fire, if you want."

"Thanks, that sounds great."

He grabbed her bags and led her down the corridor to the bedrooms, choosing the one closest to his own. "You've got your own bathroom," he told her. "I'll bring you some towels."

"I'm sorry for all the trouble," she said.

"Hey, I insisted, right? I even threw my weight around. No pity for me."

"You know what? You're absolutely right. Be inconvenienced, Zack. The more trouble I am to you, the better. I need Egyptian cotton for the sheets and at least three nonallergenic pillows. Cool-toned solid colors for the bedding, please. No busy prints."

He laughed at her. "I'm going to regret saying that to you."

"Oh, I'll make sure of it," she purred.

Oh, whoa. The husky laughter in her voice made his body tighten and throb.

Four

Every damn thing that came out of her mouth felt flirtatious. The subtext was always, *I want to ride you off into the sunset, you big hot hunk of burning love.*

Maybe it was just sexual deprivation. She didn't even know how long it had been since she had sex. At all, let alone good sex. Her last boyfriend had gotten all huffy and offended when she wouldn't stay the night, and when she finally did give it a shot, he'd been freaked out by her constant nightmares. As usual. Par for the course.

At a certain point, it just got too depressing to keep track of data like that. Better to measure life by different metrics. Concentrate on other things.

She turned her attention to his guest bedroom, which was a pretty, harmonious room. Simple, high ceilinged, with a big, gorgeous window that showed a broad expanse of city lights glowing in the distance. A queen-size wooden bed dominated the room. There was a standing mirror, an old-fashioned antique wardrobe, a matching dark wood dresser. There was even an old washstand with a pitcher and a washbasin. She'd bet good money that Zack Austin had not chosen those items.

Zack came back moments later with a heap of bedding in his arms and laid it on the wing-back chair. "Solid-tone slate-blue Egyptian cotton," he told her. "No busy prints."

"Thanks," she said. "You are aware, of course, that I was joking."

He grinned. "I'm not taking any chances. The thread count is high, I promise."

She rolled her eyes. "Oh, shut up."

"Here are towels for you, and take this, too, just in case." He laid a charcoal-gray fleece bathrobe down on top of the pile. "It's mine, so it'll be huge on you, but if you get cold, you can wrap yourself in it. That big front room out there is slow to heat up."

"Thank you," she said. "Very thoughtful of you."

"Now let me get this bed made," he said.

"Oh, don't be silly. I can handle making my own bed."

"I can handle it better," he told her. "I was a marine. I can make a bed as tight as a drum in record time."

"Well, damn. Don't hurt yourself. You don't have to bounce a quarter off it."

It was a pleasing spectacle, watching a big, athletic man lean and bend and twist and stretch, getting all the bedding shipshape.

"Great bedroom set," she said. "Very pretty. Did you pick out the furniture?"

He shot her a grin as he plumped up the pillows and sent them soaring up to the head of the bed. "Hell, no, as I'm sure you guessed. I flew Joanna and my mom out here when I got the place and gave them my credit card. They went hog wild. They got me the couches and chairs in the living room, the dining set, the bedroom sets. There's a kids' room, for when my nieces and nephew come to visit. Bunk beds, dressers, lamps."

"They did a great job," she said. "They must be so proud of you."

"Yeah, well. We're all proud of each other. So, have I forgotten anything, as your gracious host? Anything else you need from me?"

Loaded question. Ava looked over the bed. It looked great, with the puffy duvet, the heaped pillows at the head. *All that's missing is you stretched out in it, stark naked.*

She coughed. "Looks great," she said. "Thanks so much. You've been lovely."

"Okay, then. Come on out for a drink whenever you're ready. Would you like a glass of wine, or would you rather have a cocktail? I can make you a screwdriver, a gin and tonic. Or a margarita."

Her face flushed hot. "Um, no. Some wine would be fine."

"Red or white?"

"Red, please."

"Then I'll get out of your way and let you settle in."

When she was alone in the room, Ava sank down onto the bed, heart pounding.

Yikes. If he'd mentioned margaritas, then he had to be thinking about that night, too. That crazy, embarrassing night that made her feel so compromised and vulnerable.

She craved some kind of armor. Fortunately, she'd brought some with her. Those hideous pajamas were just the thing. Sexless, shapeless comfort. She dug into her suitcase and put on the oversize plaid jammies. Over them she layered the big gray fleece bathrobe that Zack had left for her. Fuzzy yellow house socks with plastic antislip soles completed the carefully curated look, which could only be described as "walking fuzz ball."

She came padding silently out of the bedroom and found him crouched in front of the fire, in jeans and a waffle-weave thermal sweatshirt. Looking great in them.

He turned to look. The expression in his eyes, for just an instant, looked territorial.

It was just a flash, a gut feeling, and it could be her imagination, but she sensed that he liked having maneuvered her into this. He liked having her right here, in his space, in her nightclothes. Swathed in his very own bathrobe. Under his protection.

Whew. Scary thought. But even scarier was the corollary realization.

She liked it, too.

Oh, man. This was so bad. She had to walk this back.

"The robe looks good on you," he said. "Come sit over here, close to the fire."

Ava did so, curling her feet up and accepting the goblet of dark red wine that he offered her. He opened a chest behind the couch, shook out a fluffy blanket in deep shades of burgundy and blue, and laid it over her, tucking it in on either side. "I have three of these in the chest," he confessed. "This is the first time I've used one."

"Let me guess," she said, sipping her wine. "Your mom and Joanna got you those couch throws, right?"

"You found me out," he said.

"They're gorgeous," she said, stroking them. "So soft. Cashmere?"

"I expect so." He sat down on the couch, a careful distance away from her, and they stared into the now roaring fire for a while.

"I guess we should be discussing your troll problem," he said. "But it's been a long day. I've looped in the cybersecurity team. We'll pick it up when we get back from your trade fair, after they've done some research, and dig into it then."

"Yes, I'd rather not dwell on it right now," she said. "It's been an intense day, and this time of year sucks for me even without my trolls."

She regretted the words the instant they came out of her mouth when she saw curiosity sharpen in his eyes. "Oh, yeah? Why is that?"

Damn. Why had she blurted that out? She never talked about it. She stalled, rolling the swallow of wine around in her mouth. "No particular reason," she mumbled.

"Don't shine me on," he said. "You have to tell me now. And you wouldn't have set me up to be curious like that if some part of you didn't want to."

Ava dug her hands into the cashmere fuzz, trying to warm them. "The fourth of this month is the anniversary of my parents' plane crash," she admitted reluctantly. "It hits me really hard, every year. Some years I handle it better than others. Sometimes I fool myself into thinking I'm cool. That I beat it this time. And then, whammo, it takes me down. I get so low, it scares me."

"I'm so sorry," he said. "How old were you when it happened?"

"Almost thirteen," she said.

He winced. "Oh, God, Ava. That's awful."

"Yeah. It left a mark."

The silence after felt more peaceful, oddly enough. She'd gotten it outside of herself. She listened to the flames crackle, feeling like more air was going into her lungs.

"I know how it feels, to have a big hole in that part of my life where a parent should be," Zack said. "But I had Granddad. He made all the difference in the world. He filled the spot where my dad should've been. When he died..." Zack shook his head. "It was like I couldn't breathe, for a month."

"Yeah," she whispered. "Yeah, I felt that way, too."

"You call someone to be with you when you feel like that, right?" he asked her. "You don't tough it out all by yourself? Tell me you don't."

"It doesn't occur to me to reach out," she said. "I'm not fit for company."

"Who cares if you're fit for company? It's not about that. You stay all alone?" Zack sounded scandalized. "That's terrible. You should ask for help. You don't have to be so damn macho about it. It's okay to reach out."

"Yeah?" she shot back. "You know what, Zack? You're macho, too. And I bet you absolutely suck at reaching out when you feel like crap. So don't preach to me."

Zack smiled. "You've got me there. Maybe reaching out isn't my most shining talent. But I have Drew and Vann, and having them makes me stronger. If I was messed up about anything, they'd help me out."

"Good," she said. "I'm glad for you. You're very fortunate."

He kept on frowning, like he wanted something more. "What about Drew?" he asked. "Can't you call on him when you're in that state?"

"Drew understands," she said. "But it's his grief and loss, too. He's sad himself on that day, on his own account, so I try to let him be."

"And Jenna?"

A rush of old memories made her smile. "Jenna, yes," she admitted. "That was how we bonded, freshman year in college. We didn't hit it off at all at first. I thought she was a stuck-up nerd with no sense of humor, and she thought I was a frivolous, spoiled diva. We were like cats and dogs. Then one day, she came back to the dorm room and found me crying in the dark. She wouldn't let up until I told her that it was the anniversary of their plane crash. Then she told me about her brother, Chris, dying, and we finally opened up to each other. Now she's my best friend in the world."

"Well, then," he said. "So you do have someone."

"Yeah. She just happens to be a half a world away, on a blissful honeymoon with my big brother. Which is great, but life's funny. It never works out like you'd expect."

He hesitated. "You could call me, too. I don't know

how much help I'd be, but I'd sure as hell show up. And I wouldn't expect you to be good company."

Ava cupped the glass with both her hands, gazing into the red liquid, too shy to meet his eyes. "That's very sweet of you," she said, her voice small. "And funny you should say that. Because, actually, you already have done that for me."

Zack's eyes narrowed in puzzlement. "How so?"

"That night," she said. "Remember? Six years ago? The margaritas?"

He inhaled sharply, eyes widening. "Oh. Holy shit."

"Yeah. It was their death anniversary that night," she said. "I didn't want to feel those feelings, so I tried to hold them off with alcohol. And distract myself with, ah…"

"Me," he finished.

The silence stretched out. Just the sound of the fire.

"I wish I'd known," he said finally.

"I wanted to tell you for a long time. I didn't want you to think that I was a habitual drunk. Or…you know. A sex addict. I'm really not."

"I never thought that," he assured her. "Not for one second."

"Thanks for saying that. Even so, I've wanted to apologize to you ever since."

"What?" He sounded shocked. "What for?"

"You know, for putting you in a compromising position. My brother is your best friend since forever. Plus, he's your boss. It just wasn't right to do that to you."

"All the more reason I'm glad nothing happened," he said.

Ava could have sworn she didn't change the expression on her face, but Zack felt the truth in the air. He looked over at her sharply.

"Wait," he said. "Hold on. You didn't know that nothing happened? You actually thought that I would… God, Ava, what kind of scumbag do you think I am?"

"I didn't know," she protested. "How could I know? I blacked out. When I woke up, you were gone. I missed my chance to ask what happened. After that, I was too mortified to ask. And the more time went by, the more mortified I got."

He closed his eyes, shaking his head. "Damn. I can't believe this."

"So, um." She cleared her throat. "Since I don't remember, please tell me. What did happen? Exactly?"

"You kissed me," he said. "And then you started to cry."

Ava winced. "Oh, no."

"I carried you to the bed and held you while you cried it out. After a while, you stopped crying and started snoring. I covered you up and slept on the couch. End of story."

"You must have thought I was crazy," she whispered.

"No," he corrected. "I thought you were sad. And very, very drunk."

Ava drank the last swallow of her wine and put the empty glass on the coffee table. "I apologize for falling all over you," she said. "It must have been embarrassing."

"No," he said. "But it was a challenge when you kissed me. To do the right thing."

Ava's face must have been cherry red, but it was

gratifying to hear that he was not completely immune to her charms. "Then why did you push me away?"

He gave her a narrow look. "Like hell. You were drunk. I knew exactly what Drew would think. Also how I would feel if it were Joanna in your situation. Alone with some guy who could take advantage if he felt like it. No way would I ever do that to someone."

"You're a good guy," she said. "But then, I knew that. Always have."

He shrugged. "Plus, it sucks to be somebody's moment of bad judgment."

"Whose bad judgment?" she asked. "What are you talking about?"

His eyes slid away from hers. "Never mind. Just stupid old stuff."

"Don't you even," she said. "You make me spit out the painful, embarrassing things." She poked at his thick-muscled shoulder with her fingertips. "It's your turn."

He shrugged. "I know how it feels to be someone's big mistake. A choice she's not proud of. Been there, done that. Never want to do it again."

She was mystified. "Who on earth would ever see you that way?"

Zack grabbed the wine, refilling their glasses and handing hers back. "It was back when I was still in the marines. I'd gone to check on a wounded friend in a military hospital in Germany. I had some leave, so I traveled. Met this girl in Berlin. Aimee. She was doing a semester abroad to study art and architecture. A debutante from Dallas. Her daddy had oil wells."

"All right," she said. "And?"

"I fell pretty hard," he said. "I wanted to make it work with her. One day she ghosted me and went off to Prague. Like an idiot, I followed her. I should have followed my own rule. If she was making such a big effort to avoid me, I should've let her do it."

"Did you find her?"

"Yes," he said. "She tried to be nice, but there's no way to sugarcoat some things. I had no money, no college degree, no connections. I was just a big, dumb, overgrown, backwoods jarhead to her. She didn't see a future in it."

She sucked in air, infuriated. "That snobbish bitch."

"She was just being honest," he pointed out. "I thought you liked honesty."

"That's not honesty. That's arrogance. Ignorance. She had no idea who she was dealing with. No freaking clue what you were capable of. She only saw herself."

Zack waved that away. "Doesn't matter. It was a long time ago. But it left a mark."

Ava studied his profile. The stunning, chiseled angles and lines and planes of his cheekbones and jaw. She wished she could lean over and touch them with her fingertips.

"If you ran into Aimee again, she'd see you very differently now," she said.

"Maybe so. But the changes are just cosmetic. The only difference is years of hard work. Bigger skill set, bigger bank account, better wardrobe. But I'm still that guy."

"The guy she couldn't see," Ava said. "But neither do you. I think there's quite a disconnect between the man everyone else sees and your own vision of yourself."

"Oh, yeah? How's that?"

"Your staff loves you and fears you," she said. "Drew and Vann just plain love you. The company founders respect you, both Uncle Malcolm and Hendrick Hill. And now that Drew and Vann are both taken, you are the last, desperate hope of the single ladies at Maddox Hill. Behold, the last of the Maddox Hill heartthrobs left standing."

He snorted under his breath. "Oh, get out of here."

"True thing. While Aimee the brain-dead debutante is probably married to some dull, self-important Dallas businessman who's bad in bed. Which is exactly what she deserves."

Zack laughed. "I never let my imagination go that far. To be honest, I can't quite remember what she looks like."

"Good," Ava said savagely.

"That said, I still don't ever want to be anybody's embarrassing mistake again," he said. "And you know what? I'm not the only one with a big disconnect."

She tensed, bracing herself for God knew what. "I don't know what you mean."

"You said today that you like it when people like you. Well, guess what? They do. You're everybody's friend. You have a million friends. The whole damn city loves you."

"Oh, don't exaggerate. What are you getting at?"

He pressed on. "But you won't call any of them to help you with grieving your anniversary date. Or even just to vent about your troll problem. You're everybody's friend, but you won't let anyone be yours."

"That's nonsense," she snapped. "I'm close to a lot of friends. And Jenna is—"

"Jenna is another matter, and she's also out of the

country. No, I'm talking about the rest of the teeming multitudes. You couldn't call on any of them. Could you?"

"Well, I called on you, didn't I?"

He studied her for a long moment. "Yes." His voice was soft. "You called on me."

The air somehow turned electric. A shimmer of awareness got sharper and sharper, until suddenly, it was unbearable. She leaned forward, placing the wineglass on the coffee table. It rattled and almost fell. She steadied it with shaking hands.

"So, ah…yeah," she mumbled. "It's been a really long day, and I should—"

"Ava," he broke in.

She swallowed nervously. "Yes?"

"Something you should know."

"Well, then," she said. "Go on. Let's hear it."

"If you should ever end up in my bed for real? You wouldn't spend years wondering whether it happened or not."

"Zack, I'm so sorry about that. Really, I blacked out. I didn't mean to imply—"

"You'd remember every last second of it." His voice was silky. "I guarantee it."

Ava threw off the cashmere blanket and got to her feet, almost tripping over the overlong bathrobe. "Um, yes," she forced out. "Understood. 'Night."

She hiked up the bathrobe and fled.

Five

At a quarter to 5:00 a.m., coffee was brewing and bacon sizzled in the pan when Zack sensed that he wasn't alone. He turned to see Ava in the entryway to the corridor, fully dressed in jeans and a red sweater, hair twisted up onto her head. Her jacket was on, her suitcase and garment bag piled behind her, and her smartphone was in her hand.

From the guilty look on her face, she'd been planning to slip away before he woke.

He'd spooked her last night, with the inappropriate comments. Jerk move.

"I'm going with you to LA," he told her. "I'm not leaving you alone until I have a team in place to cover you. Until then, I'm reporting for duty."

Ava let out a sharp sigh. "Zack, please. Be reasonable."

"Call Ernest," he said. "Tell him we'll meet him at the gate."

Ava's mouth was tight. Their fireside chat had made things worse between them, not better. Too damn much information, and she didn't know how to process it. Plus, she was embarrassed to show vulnerability. It made her defensive and cranky.

He needed to back off. Keep it classy and professional. This girl was Drew's little sister. Malcolm's niece. The Maddox family's golden princess. Even after a decade of friendship, trust and mutual esteem, he wasn't sure he wanted to know how Drew and Malcolm would feel about Zack raising his eyes to their precious Ava.

Not that his eyes had any choice. Or certain other body parts, for that matter.

"I'd rather do my thing today alone, no distractions," she told him. "We have a lot to accomplish."

Zack flicked a drop of water onto the buttered-up griddle to see if it danced. "Whatever you want," he said, pouring out the pancakes. "It's nine hours ahead in Positano, so Malcolm should pick up when I call. Don't know about Drew, but wherever he is in the world, he'll forgive me for waking him up when I tell him about your trolls."

"Bullying is not a winning strategy, Zack."

"If you really want to feel bullied, I can't stop you," he said. "It won't change my behavior. I am staying with you until another bodyguard I trust is covering you. So let me accompany you, or else discuss the issue directly with your uncle and brother."

"You know damn well they'll both overreact," she said.

"No," Zack replied. "They'll feel as I do, and I could use the moral support. This issue is spot-on when it comes to my mission. Which is to keep you all safe."

Ava's eyes slid away. "I appreciate your zeal, but this is over-the-top."

"I'd rather err on the side of caution. I'll stay out of your way. I won't mess with your process. Call Ernest and let him know. How many slices of bacon do you want?"

"Oh, give me three," she snapped. "Fighting gives me an appetite."

"I'm not fighting," he called after her as she left the kitchen. "Just stating facts."

"You hush up. Your carrot-and-stick routine is bugging me."

He heard Ava murmuring into her phone in the other room. A few moments later, she came back into the kitchen. "How is it you're awake at this ungodly hour, anyhow?"

"I grew up on my granddad's farm in West Virginia," he told her. "We got up early to take care of the livestock. Then I joined the military. It doesn't matter how late I get to bed. I can't sleep late. Usually I go running or else work out at this hour."

Ava gestured at the stove. "Smells good. What's cooking?"

"Pancakes. Gotta keep my strength up. The carrot-and-stick routine burns a lot of calories. Get yourself some coffee. Cream's on the table. Hope you like it strong."

A couple minutes later, Zack set two plates with stacks of buttermilk pancakes on the table.

Ava drizzled syrup on hers and took a bite. "Wow. So fluffy. These are fabulous."

"Mom's recipe," he said.

"You're a man of many talents," she said, forking up another bite. "I'm usually not hungry in the morning. I mean, not at all. But this…mmm. So good."

"I'm no gourmet chef, but Mom made sure I could handle the basics."

Ava tucked in her breakfast, eyeing him as she nibbled her bacon. "Won't they miss you at Maddox Hill today? Don't you have a job? A life?"

"Sure, but I'm always working, except when I fly home to see Mom and Joanna and the kids, so I almost never take vacation or personal leave days. Amelia knows what to do. If they have issues, they'll call me. The stuff I was going to do can be pushed off. So I'm clear. Both my calendar and my conscience."

"So you finally take up a hobby, and it involves helicoptering me," she said sourly. "I hope you're packed, because it's time to scram if we want to catch this flight."

"I'm all packed," he said.

Ava dabbed at her mouth with a napkin. "Thanks for breakfast. Can I help with the dishes?"

"Don't worry about it. The cleaning service is coming this morning, and they'll take care of it."

The drive to the airport was quiet. Ava shut down any attempt he made at polite conversation, and after a while he let the effort go. If she wanted to be pissed at him, that was her privilege. But as they approached the airport, the words just popped out.

"You don't have to be so defensive with me," he announced.

She looked over at him, startled. "Excuse me?"

"The stuff you said yesterday," he said. "Feeling sad about your parents. Getting trashed on margaritas. Being scared of the shitty trolls. It doesn't mean you're weak. It just means you're human, and it's okay to be human."

"Oh." She chewed on her lip. "Um… I'm not sure where that came from, but— Whoa, whoa, whoa, yikes! Zack, you just passed the exit for our terminal!"

Zack cursed under his breath as he glanced at the exit in the rearview mirror and resolved to shut his great big mouth before he hurt himself.

They left Zack's car in the parking garage and powered through the whole airport process in grim silence. Ernest was already at the gate, and the younger guy's cheerful, nonstop chatter effectively covered up the tense silence between them.

As soon as the plane was airborne, Ava and Ernest fired up their laptops, but after a while, Ernest leaned over and tapped Zack's sleeve.

"Have you seen Ava's videos?"

"Ernest, don't bug him," Ava said. "It's not his—"

"I've seen the one about Arm's Reach," Zack said. "It was excellent. There are more?"

"Oh, yeah. She's done loads of them, and they always go viral. She's, like, a wizard that way. We're in the middle of producing a big one about the Blooms and the Desert Bloom Farm. Ava always narrates, because she's awesome at it."

"Ernest!" Ava protested. "Don't put him on the spot! He may not be interested."

"I am interested, very. Show me, please," Zack said.

"Okay. Check this out," Ernest said, passing over his laptop. "This is the first section of the Desert Bloom bit, and it'll run on one of the interactive video screens in the booth at the trade show. Put in your earphones."

Zack calmly ignored Ava's efforts to excuse him from watching, hooked himself up and settled in to watch. A minimalist fingerpicking guitar piece accompanied drone footage, swooping over a huge swath of desert. It was dry and bare, just a few scrubby thorns clinging to life, as Ava's clear, golden voice narrated the story of two pioneers of modern botany and soil research, most appropriately named the Blooms. How, by pure chance, some years ago they inherited a tract of arid desert in Southern California and decided to turn it green using their skills as biologists. Replenishing the depleted soil bacteria and fungi, refilling the aquifers. Then, with startling abruptness, the drone footage showed the desert turning green. The land was suddenly thick with long grass, bushes and small trees. Then the drone swooped over orchards, gardens, greenhouses.

Damn, he could listen to her gorgeous voice forfreaking-ever. So sexy.

The drone flew lower, along a meandering stream, then over a pond, where a flock of birds took flight as she talked about soil biota. How its symbiotic relationship with plants facilitated uptake of soil minerals. How fungi stabilized the soil against erosion by forming water-stable aggregates. How the Blooms' process of soil inoculation worked.

He watched to the end of the clip, pulled out his earbuds and looked at Ava.

"Incredible project," he said. "They're up for a cash prize?"

"Yeah, half a million," she said. "It's a drop in the bucket, but every little bit counts. I've also been trying to get Drew to meet with them, to talk about Beyond Earth."

He was surprised by the mention of Maddox Hill's speculative futuristic project, his friend Drew's darling, geared toward possible future construction on Mars. "These guys want to go off world?"

She laughed. "Oh, they'll start with Earth. We have plenty of dry, dusty deserts here to work on. Winning the prize would be great, but the real prize is to rub elbows with investors who can take them to the next level. Please, God. I really need for this to work."

"Yeah? Have you sunk your own personal money into this project?"

"Some," she admitted. "They really need the investors, but they have to make a big splash to attract the right ones, so I'm covering the cost of the Future Innovation booth. The Blooms will pay me back when they can. They've also offered me a percentage. It's a gamble, but I think there's a big payoff in store down the line."

Zack was startled. "A booth at a trade show like that is one hell of an expense."

"Tell me about it," she said fervently. "I had to dig deep to cover it. I've been pulling down research grants for the Blooms since my college days, back when I interned at the Maddox Hill Foundation during the summers. I helped Bobby and Wilbur write their first grant application back then. If Drew hadn't been on his honeymoon right now, I would have dragged him down to meet them. The Blooms would be great partners for his carbon-sink architecture projects. Green walls, hanging gardens, green roofs to moderate temperature and make building complexes carbon negative. It'll spawn a whole new service industry. High-rise gardening."

"Yes," he said. "Drew would be excited by this project."

"And there's Beyond Earth," she went on. "Who better than the two crazy soil biologists who are turning Earth's deserts green to work on terraforming Mars?"

"You think big," Zack commented.

"I believe in the Blooms," Ava said. "Wilbur's incredible at making dirt come to life, and Bobby is a wizard with bacteria and arbuscular mycorrhizal fungi. I've been pushing this narrative for years now. Two dedicated, monk-like nerds, saving the planet one petri dish and hyphal network at a time. They have this way of coming at problems from every angle you could think of and then a hundred more that you wouldn't. The two of them are one big brain that needed more than one body to function. And anyone who partners with them will end up extremely rich, in the long run. Those guys are laser focused. Brains like a nuclear furnace."

"Like you," Zack said.

Ava seemed taken aback. "Me? Hardly!"

"Laser focused, brain like a nuclear furnace?" Zack said. "Sounds like you." He paused at the stunned look on her face. "What? Did I say something bad?"

"Ah, no," Ava said. "Just surprising. I was under

the impression that you thought I was, ah…you know. Bimbo fluff."

Zack felt his face get hot. "I'm sorry if I ever gave you that impression," he said stiffly. "Social graces haven't ever been one of my strongest points."

"More my fault than yours, most likely," Ava assured him. "Considering that night with the margaritas and all. God knows, that would make anyone feel awkward."

The phone vibrated in Zack's pocket. He pulled it out. It was Vikram, who managed the close protection agents. Zack had left a long, detailed voice mail message for him last night about the security detail they needed to set up for Ava.

He hit Talk. "Hey, Vikram."

"Zack. Sorry it took a while to get back to you, but I wanted to get the team in place before we spoke. I've got four guys who can cover her 24-7 on a rotating basis, and I've messaged you their names. They're ready now, so where is she located? Is she at the Gilchrist building or still at home?"

"Actually, she's on a plane, on her way down to Southern California right now."

"Southern California?" Vikram sounded scandalized. "On a plane? No security?"

"I'm with her on the plane," he assured Vikram. "She's covered."

"You? Uh…why you? That doesn't seem like a good use of your—"

"I took a few vacation days. I needed a change of scenery. I'll just cover her until she gets back. She's got this work thing, a trade fair in LA. We'll come back

Tuesday night. I'll be in touch. Have the team ready for Wednesday. Thanks for the names."

Vikram was speechless for a moment. "So, it's, uh… it's that kind of thing?"

"Not at all," he said hastily. "This just caught me by surprise. She had to catch an early flight, and I couldn't let her leave without having her covered, so…here I am."

"Yeah. There you are," Vikram said slowly. "You know, the guys on my roster practically clubbed each other unconscious to be first in line to guard that woman's body."

"Talk to you Wednesday, Vikram. Later." Zack ended the call before Vikram could piss him off.

Ava gave him a questioning look.

"It's Vikram, one of my guys," he explained. "He's putting together your team."

She rolled her eyes. "Oh, joy."

Once they thrashed their way through LAX, the limo took them to the new convention center and hotel in West Hollywood. Zack heard an excited yell as they walked into the huge hotel lobby. He stepped in front of Ava as two tall, gangling figures pelted toward them and then recognized the huge foreheads, thick glasses, bushy clouds of hair. Huge, crazy grins that showed off all their gums. The Blooms.

Ava stepped out from behind him to meet them. One of them grabbed her, swinging her around, which made Zack's hackles rise, but Ava was laughing and smiling. Then the other guy took his turn with the hugging and swinging. The two were a perfectly matched set. Twins maybe, or if they weren't, they might as well be.

"Zack, meet Bobby and Wilbur Bloom," Ava said. "Old friends of mine. Bobby and Wilbur, this is Zack Austin, the chief security officer at Maddox Hill. He's keeping me company while I work out my online troll problems."

"Yeah, we heard about that," Bobby said. "If we find those nasty bastards, we'll totally mulch them for you."

"Yeah," Wilbur added darkly. "We'll bury those scumbags in a crap ton of hot compost. Take 'em apart on a molecular level and repurpose freaking everything they've got. Who knows, maybe they'll eventually turn into something useful."

Ava gave them each a smacking kiss of appreciation on the cheek. "Thanks, boys. That's very gratifying. Have you gone over to the convention center to see the booth?"

"We just got here now," one of them said. "We were just about to take the van over with the plants."

"Wonderful," Ava said briskly. "Just let us check in to our rooms really quick, and we'll all head over there together."

The only holdup was a sharp disagreement with Ava about room disposition. He insisted on a room that connected with hers, which put the two of them on a different floor from the Blooms and Ernest. Zack stood his ground, despite Ava's very vocal frustration.

He was good at his job. Being accommodating or nice wasn't part of that job.

Once they got through that barrier, they headed over to the convention center and the expo floor. It looked like Times Square, with all the colorful, lit-up screens, logos and displays, and the bustle of preparation for tomorrow.

Desert Bloom's booth was in a prized central location, so Ava must be paying dearly for the space. The interactive screens in the booth were up and running, so while Ava and the Blooms set up finishing touches and installed live plant displays, Zack situated himself where he could see Ava, stuck in his earbuds and listened to the presentation on the screen. Ava's caressing voice described the Blooms' game-changing work with bacteria and fungi and explained how the Earth's deserts could be made fertile, replenishing aquifers, producing food, supporting ecosystems, protecting biodiversity. By the time she got to the part about sequestering carbon, he was half aroused.

Whoever would have thought that soil biology could be so damn stimulating?

Six

Stop it. Just stop it. Right now.

The silent lecture wasn't working as well as usual. Ava had way too much to accomplish today to indulge in this nonsense. From the moment they arrived to check in at the convention hotel, Zack had been bugging her. On her nerves. In her face.

First that stupid fight over the hotel rooms. Weeks ago, she'd asked for a room next to Bobby, Wilbur and Ernest. Today, Zack had insisted on a room that connected with hers internally. Which necessitated being on a different floor from her crew. Not ergonomic at all, but when she put up a fight, he trotted out his usual big bully stick. The awful, dreaded call to Uncle Malcolm and Drew. Oh, the terror. His ploy worked, though, because she did not want to deal with a scolding rant from her brother and uncle on top of her other stress. So Zack won that fight.

This trade show was incredibly important, for the Blooms and for her, and she did not have extra thought cycles to spare for a brooding hunk who followed her around watching everything she did, overhearing everything she said, examining everyone she talked to. It was unsettling. Embarrassing. People were starting to notice. And speculate.

She tried so hard to project confidence, to appear put-together, competent, at the top of her game. It functioned like a force field. Shields up, and off she went. It worked, for the most part. People paid attention and hopped to it. Stuff got done.

But when Zack Austin looked at her, her force field vanished, like it didn't exist and never had. It didn't matter what she was doing or wearing. Whether she was in hideous oversize pajamas and a cashmere couch throw, or a power suit, or jeans and a sweater and boots, like today, his gaze made her feel naked.

The sensation was disturbingly intimate. She'd never felt anything like it. Not even with past lovers. And the constant tingle of sexual awareness didn't help, either. He looked so damn good, standing around with his muscular arms crossed over his barrel chest, looking suspicious. Protective. And handsome.

Frantic activity dampened down the anxiety, which was one of the reasons she always worked so hard. It was a family trait, of course, one she shared with Drew and her uncle, but working hard kept the howling emptiness at bay while getting tons of stuff accomplished.

She could look at that situation as a win-win, if she squinted a little bit.

When they arrived this afternoon, Henly and Frank, her trade show associates, had already set the booth up. She'd worked with them for years. She designed the trade show booth concepts, layout, sales literature and show apps, and Henly and Frank developed her ideas and brought them to life. They did all the construction, furniture, graphics, interactive screens, storage, transport, setup and teardown, and they did it well.

The brand-new booth looked great. All that was left were finishing touches, like Bobby and Wilbur's more delicate plant exhibits that had to be set up at the last minute, and the catering, of course. The goodies served tomorrow were sustainably sourced from Bobby and Wilbur's Desert Bloom Farm, all made from crops grown on land the brothers had reclaimed from the arid desert. There would be freshly baked artisanal crackers with assorted pâtés made from sun-dried tomatoes, artichokes and olives. There would be wines from Bobby and Wilbur's vineyards, mojitos made with lemons from their orchard, and mint from their herb garden.

They had to kick butt at this show, for Bobby and Wilbur's sake. And for hers, too. Aside from the rental of the space and the juice required to run it, she was personally on the hook for Carl and Henly's latest bill, and it was a biggie. The snack bar and drinks for three days of free goodies weren't cheap, either, but it was all part of her wicked plan—sink Desert Bloom name recognition deep into the viewing public's fickle brains by assaulting all five of their senses with pleasure and delight. And alcohol, of course.

She could stomach the risk, and she was confident that she'd make her money back, plus a huge profit in the long run. But she needed to keep the Blooms absolutely on track, which would be a challenge. It was up to her to keep all the plates spinning in the air, and for that she needed focus. No sexy, brooding, smoldering distractions allowed.

Ten o'clock had come and gone, and Bobby and Wilbur were still fussing over their pet plants, so she gave them the usual big-sisterly lecture about eating something and getting enough sleep and left them to it. Frank and Henly had already gone off to the hotel to crash, and Ernest had left earlier to have dinner with a friend.

But Zack was still there, patiently waiting. While working, she could stay busy and focused enough to ignore him, but now she'd suddenly gone all breathless and fluttery again. It made her so irritated at herself. Reacting like a hormonal adolescent.

Zack joined her as she left the booth, walking alongside her out of the big convention center.

"It's late," she told him. "You must be hungry. You could have just gone ahead and gotten yourself dinner hours ago, you know."

He grunted. "That would entirely defeat the purpose of being here."

"I was never alone," she told him. "And really, Zack. I'm not in physical danger."

"I hope you're correct, and I'll continue to hope that while I watch your back at all times. And Vikram will have a team ready when we get back to Seattle to keep that up."

She winced. "Oh, God. You mean day and night? For real?"

"Absolutely. Until we are all satisfied that you are no longer in danger."

She contemplated that grim and inconvenient prospect as they strolled through the balmy Los Angeles evening and into the adjacent luxury hotel that housed the convention center's participants. The hotel had two towers, with an open outdoor space with a large swimming pool between them. The restaurant's open-air seating was on a second-floor terrace that overlooked the pool. Their rooms were in the second tower. A couple of teenagers were horsing around in the pool as they walked past it down the breezeway.

"Are you hungry?" Zack asked her. "The restaurant should still be serving."

"I'm too buzzed to eat," Ava told him. "I get that way when I'm on the road. Maybe I'll order something later. Please, feel free to grab some dinner on your own. I don't want to stop you from eating."

He let out a noncommittal grunt. "I'll see you to your room."

They entered the lobby of the second hotel tower and headed toward the elevator banks, and Ava heard a voice behind her.

"Ava? Ava Maddox? Is that you?"

Ava turned to see a familiar face approaching, a big, toothy smile spread over it, arms wide for a hug. Craig Redding, a man she'd known from college. She'd been briefly involved with him years ago, but it hadn't taken even her young-and-dumb self very long to conclude that the relationship had no future. Craig was smart and good-looking, even if his eyes were pinched a little too close together, but on closer acquaintance, he'd proved to be arrogant and condescending. The Reddings were vastly rich and well-connected, and Craig had grown up convinced that he was God's gift. He had expected her to be grateful for his attentions. The memory made her neck hairs prickle up.

However, the Reddings had also commissioned Maddox Hill to design several large buildings for them, and when that much money was involved, Malcolm had made it clear that she was expected to smile and nod like a good little girl.

Up until now, she'd managed to do so from a safe distance.

Zack stepped in front of her, effectively blocking Craig's move to embrace her. "Who are you?" he demanded.

"It's fine, Zack." She came forward, but not close enough to get dragged into a hug. "I know him. We went to school together. Hey, Craig. What brings you here? I thought you worked at your dad's hedge fund in Portland."

"I have my own venture capital firm now," Craig told her. "I make the rounds of the tech trade fairs to keep my finger on the pulse of the future. What is it you do these days? Aren't you some kind of social media influencer? Like, what? Instagram videos? Makeup, fashion, that kind of thing? Cat memes and all that?"

She smiled, teeth clenched. "Hey, someone's got to do it."

"Branding communication specialist is the best description for what she does, I'd say," Zack said. "But she wears so many hats, I can't even keep track of them all."

Ava was taken aback at his contribution. The elevator dinged and opened.

Craig waved his key card. "I'm going up, too. Share a ride?"

Zack's face darkened, but there was no socially acceptable way of refusing him, so they all got in. The elevator door sighed closed.

"So who's your friend, Ava?" Craig's voice got that insinuating tone that had always annoyed her.

Zack's voice never had that tone when he spoke to her. He was so straightforward. An odd reflection to find herself making, but whatever. "Craig Redding, meet Zack Austin," she said. "Zack is the chief security officer of Maddox Hill Architecture."

Craig's eyebrows shot up. "Really? I took him for a bodyguard. He has the look."

"I expect he does," Zack said coolly. "He's here to make sure that Ava's not bothered by anyone she doesn't feel like talking to."

"Aw. There, there. Ava and I are old friends." Craig's big white teeth were on full display. "You don't have to puff out your chest with me, buddy."

The elevator dinged and opened. Ava stepped out, followed by Zack, grateful that this wasn't Craig's floor. She didn't particularly want Craig to have her room number.

"'Night, Craig," she crisply. "See you around tomorrow at the trade show."

When the door closed, she blew out a breath of relief. "Sorry about that," she muttered. "Craig's kind of a jerk."

"I noticed," he said. "Cat memes? For real?"

"Yeah, Craig never took me seriously, but God knows I was used to that, after all those years with Uncle Malcolm." She stopped at her door. "Anyhow. Good night."

She swiped her card, but Zack made no move toward his own door. His eyes looked troubled. "Malcolm really does that to you? He puts you down, like that guy?"

"Uncle Malcolm doesn't get the point of what I do, so he dismisses it as frivolous," she said. "I gave up looking for validation from him a long time ago. He loves me, in his clumsy way, and he knows I work hard. He just would really, really rather that I was an architect. That, he could appreciate. It's the only thing that makes sense to him."

"I wish he could see what I saw today," Zack said. "How well you work. The videos, too. You're damned talented at what you do."

"Ah…wow. Thanks," she said, flustered. "Um. Good night."

Once inside the room, that connecting door loomed large in her mind. Zack had used dirty tricks to get her into this situation, but this was new, and the dirtiest trick of all. Saying sweet, approving things to her about her professional skills? That was diabolical. He'd get her eating right out of his hand in no time, the sneaky bastard.

It was a new, crafty element of his Ava management strategy. That old carrot-and-stick routine. If the threat to call Drew and Uncle Malcolm home early from their traveling was the stick, then admiring compliments about her skill and talent must be the carrot.

And she was so hungry for approval, she fell like an overripe pear, ker-plop.

Screw it. She flipped through the hotel info for the pool hours. She had to blow off some steam, and swimming worked best if she wanted a hope in hell of sleeping. Sleep was always elusive for her, even when she wasn't challenged by menacing cybertrolls and a smoldering Zack Austin. Exercise made the nightmares ease off, too. A little bit.

The pool was open until late, so she dug out her bathing suit and her flip-flops. She twisted her hair back into a braid and then sat on the bed and listened intently for Zack's movements in the connecting room. She stopped short of putting her ear to the door, because that would be creepy. It was weird enough already to be listening for him, like a teenaged girl making to sneak out for a night of misbehavior.

She already felt acutely vulnerable with Zack Austin, even when she was fully clothed, made up and coiffed. She couldn't imagine how it would feel to have him see her naked, wet, dripping and shivering. No way. She couldn't. She would implode.

She pulled the door open and gasped to find Ernest standing right there, his big eyes wide and startled behind his glasses. "Hi," he said.

"You could have knocked!" she whispered fiercely.

"I was going to, but you beat me to it," Ernest whispered back. "Why are we whispering?"

"Shh." She glanced toward Zack's door. "I was just

popping down for a quick swim, and I wanted to do it in blessed privacy. What do you need, Ernest?"

"Your computer," he told her. "Remember that invoice we needed to correct, for that extra interactive panel? I was supposed to fix that and send the corrected invoice back to Carl yesterday, but I spaced out. Now I need to get it from your computer, fix it and send it to him pronto. He needs it tomorrow morning. Sorry to bug you."

"All right. Come on in." Ava stepped back to let him in and pulled her pink laptop out of the case, opening it up. "I just got here, so I haven't set up the Wi-Fi password yet."

"I'll do it." Ernest's voice remained a conspiratorial whisper as he eyed the connecting door. "I know your logins. Go on down, get your swim. I'll be quick."

"You sure you don't need me?"

"Not at all," he assured her. "Go on, go on. Close the door quietly."

She followed his suggestion and ran down the hall toward the elevator. This was childish, but a few dozen laps in that pool and she'd be able to make it through the night.

More or less. With a little luck, and fingers crossed. Even with Zack Austin fulminating silently on the other side of an unlocked door.

Zack jerked his tie loose as he ran his eyes over the room service menu. He wondered if he dared to knock on the door and suggest that they eat together. Ava was so mercurial. Sometimes blazing that warm, generous energy straight at him, dazzling him. Then, just as fast, bam, she barricaded herself, and it felt like a door slamming in his face.

He had just decided to act like a professional adult and leave her the hell alone when he heard the room door next to his, falling to with a heavy thud.

What the hell? She wasn't supposed to leave without him in attendance. He lunged for his own door and looked out in both directions. No one was in the corridor, so he went to the connecting door and rapped on it.

"Ava?" he called. "Hey! Ava, are you in there? Everything good in there?"

No response. He knocked again, louder.

Still nothing. He banged on it. "Damn it, Ava! Answer me!"

When she still didn't answer, he cursed under his breath and shoved the door open.

Ava wasn't in the room. It was Ernest at the desk, tapping at Ava's laptop. He had earbuds on and was beating time with his feet to a song only he could hear.

"Ernest? What are you doing here?"

Ernest made no sign of hearing him, so Zack strode over to the desk and slammed his hand down on the surface, making the laptop rattle and bounce.

Ernest jumped, letting out a startled squeak, and popped out his earbuds. "Oh my flipping God! You scared me practically to death!"

"Where is Ava? And why are you in her room?"

"I just needed to use her computer!" Ernest yelled. "Jeez! Calm down!"

"Where is she?" Zack demanded.

"She went down for a swim, that's all. She always does that when we go on the road. Otherwise she can't sleep. She has insomnia, and it gets really bad sometimes."

"A *swim*?" Zack's voice cracked in outrage.

He strode over to the window and yanked the curtain back, peering down into the central space at the huge pool ten floors below, surrounded by deserted deck chairs.

No one down there at all but a single slim figure, knifing swiftly through the water.

Goddamn. He clenched and flexed his hands, fighting the fury and frustration.

He looked over at Ernest, who seemed bewildered. "You should head on back to your room, Ernest. It's very late."

The younger man nodded. "Yeah. I'll just, ah, scram now. 'Night."

Zack strolled to the elevator, keeping his pace measured and his breathing even more so. He couldn't go on the offensive with her. Ava was proud and stubborn, and if he pushed her too hard, she'd tell him to piss off. Carrot and stick notwithstanding.

He didn't usually struggle to control his temper. Something about Ava crossed his wires. But the more conflict there was between them, the less safe Ava would be.

Her safety was more important than his ego.

Seven

Ava pulled herself up on the side of the pool and shoved wet hair out of her eyes. Something was in front of her, blocking the light. Her eyes came into focus on a pair of shoes. Then gray suit pants. Up, up, up…to Zack's face, looming over her. Glaring down with that patented, terrifying, lightning-and-brimstone look that only he could pull off.

"Oh," she said, dismayed. "It's you."

"That's right," he said.

Zack was standing directly in front of her, so Ava scooted over a bit before vaulting up and out of the pool. She squeezed water out of her hair as she steeled herself. She tried to project confidence and calm. A big ask while dripping and mostly naked.

"Zack," she said. "I sense that you have something to say. Let's hear it."

"You're not taking me seriously." Zack's voice vibrated with tension. "There's online info about your whereabouts this weekend. Anyone at all with an interest in you can find out where you are, and at what hotel. And you blow off your security and sneak down for a swim in a deserted pool at night? In what universe is that a sane thing to do?"

Ava sidestepped his question. "Hardly deserted," she murmured. "It was full of yelling teenagers until just a few minutes ago, and there's a stream of people up and down the breezeway. Plus the restaurant." She gestured at the terrace full of late-night diners.

Zack didn't even glance toward the restaurant or breezeway. "Why are you making this so goddamned hard?"

"I'm not," she retorted. "The hard part is all you, Zack."

As soon as the words left her mouth, she regretted them. They sounded dismissive, which he did not deserve. "Look, I'm sorry," she said. "I'll go back on up to the room. And I promise I'll be good." She turned away to get the terry-cloth robe on the deck chair.

Zack's hand shot out and clamped around her wrist.

She looked down at his big hand. Contact with his skin sent a hot thrill of pure awareness through her body. A rush of energy. Anger, and something else.

Something even bigger, wilder. More dangerous.

"You're being a bully," she said slowly. "Take your hand off me right now."

His fingers tightened around her wrist. "Stop acting like a child."

That arrogant bastard. On impulse, she twisted her

hand around to grip his wrist and pitched herself backward toward the pool.

Dragging him in along with her.

There was a huge splash, a moment of disorientation…and then disbelief as she swam up to face what she'd just done.

Holy crap. She'd just pulled Zack Austin into a swimming pool, fully clothed. Like a bad little kid. And in front of an audience, no less. Some of whom were applauding from the restaurant terrace. They had now officially become the evening's live entertainment.

Zack's head and shoulders emerged from the water, his white dress shirt clinging to every detail of his thickly muscled body. He wiped his face, eyes blazing.

"Are you fucking kidding me?" he said savagely.

Stay tough. She held herself as tall as she could, trying to match his energy.

"Never lay a hand on me in a controlling way, ever again," she told him. "Or I will mess you up so bad. Do you get me?"

A muscle pulsed in Zack's jaw. "I get you," he said.

"Good," she replied.

They stood motionless in the water, eyes locked as the sounds of the world around them retreated, leaving the two of them in a bubble of breathless silence.

"How did we get here, Ava?" he asked finally. "What the hell just happened?"

"I don't know," she said. "I… I wasn't thinking."

"That much was clear," he growled.

Ava's chin went up. "I'm not apologizing."

"I didn't ask you to," he replied. "Just be straight with

me. Do you really believe that protecting you is stupid and unnecessary?"

"No. I wouldn't have come to you in the first place if I believed that," she said.

"Then why sneak off without telling me? Where's the sense in that?"

"No sense," she admitted. "Just necessity, I guess. I reached a sort of breaking point. I had to get clear of everything for a little while."

"Clear of being protected? Secure?"

"No," she said, her voice strangled. "Clear of you."

Zack's eyes widened, and the water between them boiled as he surged back, putting more distance between them. "If I'm the problem, then this situation can't go forward," he said stiffly. "I'll call Vikram when we get upstairs. He'll send a team on the first available flight tomorrow. As soon as they're here, I'll get out of your hair."

"No! I don't want anyone but you," she blurted.

Zack looked blank. "But you just told me that I'm the problem."

"Don't call Vikram," she repeated.

Zack sank down into the water and floated there for a moment, studying her face with those intense eyes. Trying to read her. "I'm lost, Ava," he said. "Help me out here."

"I'm lost, too," she said, her voice small.

"It's because of that night of the margaritas, right?" he said. "That's what your problem is with me. You want everyone to think that you're strong, all the time. You just can't stand it if somebody sees beneath your mask."

That might be true, but she couldn't comment. Her throat quivered too hard.

Zack moved so gradually, he hardly seemed to move at all, but suddenly, he was just inches from her. The slightest movement and they would touch.

"I can't make a move," he said. "Not after that epic smackdown. I've just gotten scolded, threatened and dunked in a pool. So I'm just going to float here and wait for a signal from you. If there's something you want from me, Ava, just take it."

The tiles of the pool wall pressed against her shoulder blades. She fought for breath. "It's a terrible idea," she whispered. "Totally bonkers."

"Agreed," he said. "And yet, here we are."

"Something about you just drives me nuts," she admitted.

His mouth curved in a devastating smile. "Hmm. I can work with that."

She almost laughed, but she was too unstable emotionally to risk it. But suddenly, her shoulders were no longer pressed against the tile. She was drifting toward him.

"It's going to be hard to put this back in the box," he warned. "Just be aware."

Ava laid her hands on Zack's shoulders. Her fingers twisted into the wet, sodden cotton of his shirt, and the thick, hard muscles beneath. She let her legs float up to twine around his. "I don't want it in a box," she whispered as their lips touched.

It started small, just the lightest contact, but the magic took hold instantly. The kiss burst into full bloom. The stroke of his tongue against hers was so sweet. Electric. The tantalizing taste of him, the deep, rumbling vibration of his low moan. And then the nudge of his very thick, very substantial erection against her bare belly.

The teasing contact made her shiver and moan. Her legs tightened around his, hips pulsing for deeper contact. She twined her arms around his neck, and her hands slid into the silky short hair, as aroused as if he'd been teasing her for hours.

Because he had been. She'd been intensely sexually aware of him ever since that meeting in his office the evening before. This entire day had been one long seductive foreplay session, and it was finally time for the main event. She ached for him. All of him, all over her, deep inside her. Nothing held back.

His hand wound into her wet hair, and his lips moved softly against her mouth, exploring the shape of her mouth. "Damn," he said thickly. "Our audience."

She suddenly heard the hoots and whistles coming from the terrace of the restaurant. Some people were leaning over the railing, shouting off-color advice.

She was not an exhibitionist. It was startling to realize that she'd forgotten their existence. "Um. Wow." She hugged him closer, arms and legs. "That was intense."

"Still is," Zack said, gasping with pleasure as she squeezed her thighs around his. "Let's take this upstairs."

She slid down until her feet hit the bottom of the pool after a reluctant moment. It had taken years of waiting and a huge leap of faith, courage and madness to do this, and she didn't want to turn her back on it. It might vanish like smoke.

"I'm afraid the moment will slip away," she whispered.

"Not a problem," he said. "I've been hot for you since

you were barely more than jailbait. If you want this, it's yours. Standing at attention and awaiting your pleasure, as much as you can handle, for as long as you want. Guaranteed. Nothing will slip away."

Her face heated, but his words were the encouragement she needed. She climbed up out of the pool. Zack waited in the water as she retrieved her robe from the deck chair.

"Aren't you getting out?" she asked as she wrapped herself in it.

"I'm trying to chill down this hard-on enough to make it through the hotel lobby," he confessed. "It's tricky when your clothes are sopping wet. They cling."

Zack climbed out of the pool and strolled along beside her with a supremely casual air. As if it were perfectly normal to leave a river of water on the carpet behind him. By the time they got to the elevator, she was laughing at him.

"What?" he demanded. "What's so funny?"

"You're squelching," she murmured. "Sorry. It's just a funny sound."

Zack snorted under his breath and stepped into the elevator. Another couple moved to follow them in, took one look at the Zack, drenched and with the puddle of chlorinated water spreading around his feet, and stopped short, doubtful.

"Are you guys coming up?" Ava asked.

"We'll get the next one," the guy said as the door closed.

They exploded with stifled laughter, and Zack seized her as the elevator shot up to their floor, kissing her breathless. Ten floors just wasn't long enough for that wild kiss. It continued, frantically, outside the elevator and at intervals all the way down the hall.

At her door, Zack paused, leaning back. His breath was uneven. "You've had a minute to think about it," he said. "So where are you with this? Still with me?"

"I'm with you," she said. "I just want to get the chlorine off. A quick shower."

"You got it." He grinned at her as she swiped her card.

Once inside her room, Ava leaned on the inside of the door, shaking. This was really happening. She couldn't believe it. But she had no time to waste on disbelief.

She peeled off the bathing suit and showered, shaving her legs, washing and conditioning her hair. She went at it with the blow-dryer and the round brush until she was satisfied with the way it looked and was almost tempted to put on some mascara, but no. It was a night to be au naturel. Some scented lotion and she was done with body prep.

She pulled on her sleep stuff, wishing she'd brought something sexier. The little gray stretch cotton cami and boy shorts were nowhere near as seductive as she'd like, but they were better than the horrendous flannel she'd used as a sex repellant at Zack's house.

Then she sat down on the bed, wondering nervously if the ball was in her court now. If she should signal him. A knock on the door resolved that dilemma, thank God.

"Come in," she called.

Zack walked in barefoot, in black athletic pants that hung low on his hips. His body was big and barrel-chested. Heavily muscled, but lean and cut. "Hey," he said.

He looked uncertain, lurking by the door, so she sat

up straighter and smiled at him. “I haven’t changed my mind, if that’s what you’re wondering,” she told him.

He closed the door behind himself. “Thank God,” he said.

They just stood there, gazing at each other. “It’s been a really long time for me,” Ava told him. “I don’t know if I even remember the rules.”

“Screw the rules. We’ll make up fresh ones as we go.”

She let her eyes roam over his gorgeous chest, his dazzling smile. “Sounds good.”

“One big issue still has to be addressed,” he said. “I need to throw on a shirt and go out and hunt down some condoms. I don’t carry them on me.”

“Oh. About that,” she said. “I’ve had my bloodwork done. Several times since I was last involved with anyone. I have no diseases.”

“Same,” he said. “It’s been a while for me, too. I’m in the clear.”

“Great. In that case, you should also know that I’ve been on the pill for years. I take it to regulate my cycle. So on that account, we’re covered. You don’t need to go out looking for latex.”

Zack looked startled. “For real? You’d just trust me like that?”

Ava thought about it for a moment. “Yes,” she said with conviction. “Absolutely. You’re a straight-up guy. Honest to a fault. Even if it costs you.”

“You, too,” he said. “You never take the easy way out. I’ve seen that when I see you go toe-to-toe with Drew or Malcolm. You never back down from a fight.”

“Well, we’re good, then,” she said. “No more distractions or delays. You aren't going anywhere until I have my wicked way with you." She stood up and slowly paced over to where Zack stood. Taking her time, until she was inside the heat that emanated from him and could smell his soap, toothpaste, aftershave.

She leaned closer with a dreamy smile, hungrily inhaling his scent. "You shaved for me," she whispered. "I'm touched." She caressed the sharp points and planes of his square jaw. "Sandalwood and spices. Yum, nice. You are delicious, and I—"

Her words were lost against his fierce, ravenous kiss.

Zack took her at her word. He didn't really have a choice. This energy has been building up for so long. Ten long years. Ever since that fateful barbecue out at Vashon Island, right after he arrived in Seattle. That was the night Drew had introduced him to his stunning kid sister, who quickly became the star of all his erotic fantasies.

Finally, he was kissing her for real. Like he wanted to devour her. Like he was afraid she'd melt into smoke if he let go, turned his back.

He'd never allowed himself think beyond a hot fantasy in the privacy of his own mind. Not with this girl, not even back at the beginning. God knew, in those days he'd still been fresh off that bad scene with Aimee, in Berlin. He'd sworn off pretty, pampered princesses forever.

But Ava didn't belong in Aimee's category. Or any other category. She was unique, a force of nature. Strong and lithe and pliant in his arms, and her sweet, full lips tasted incredible. So soft. Her mouth was open to him, letting him inside, welcoming his tongue, his touch as he explored every lush detail. She wrapped her arms around his neck and dragged him closer.

He leaned back to take a look. Her gorgeous blue eyes were dilated, and her breasts were high and tilted, the tight little nipples poking through the soft, stretchy fabric of her camisole. Taut and stiff against his stroking hands. She shivered with arousal.

"Av," he whispered. "You're perfect."

"Hardly. That's sweet, but extravagant," she said. "Even so…thanks."

She was so wrong about that. She shone. Her skin was so hot and smooth. Flower-petal soft. That soft, thick hair, sliding through his fingers. Her hands gripped his shoulders, her sharp little nails digging into him as she kissed him back.

Bad kitty. No mercy. Not that he wanted any.

She leaned back for air. "I packed my sleepwear before I knew I was going to be seduced," she said breathlessly. "Or I would have brought some sexy negligée or other."

"Are you kidding me? That cute gray outfit makes me so hot, I can't breathe."

She laughed at him. "A stretch cami and boy shorts? Dude, you are easy to please."

Hell yeah, if it's you. He stopped himself from saying it out loud. Didn't want to be clingy or grabby. Too soon for big confessions. She didn't necessarily need to know that she was his benchmark for female hotness. It must have been that fateful night he'd spent lying next to her while she wept and then slept off the margaritas. That night had nailed it down for him. All those hours spent stroking her soft, silky hair, watching her sleep.

Wondering about her dreams, her thoughts. What made her so damn sad. Wishing he could fix it for her.

That night had done something to him. He was imprinted. Couldn't shake it.

That had put a hell of a damper on his love life. No one ever measured up to his fantasies. Nor was it fair to expect anyone to do so. Ava was one of a kind.

Like everyone else, of course. But he was stuck on her. No one else would do. Such a chump. His tried-and-true pattern, to fixate on a woman he could not have.

And now, here she was. Filling his eyes, his arms, his senses.

"There's a bed, you know," Ava murmured. "If you get tired of holding me up."

No danger of that, but still, the bed sounded good. He carried her over to it and sat down with her body still wrapped around his. Ava shifted, wiggling around until she was straddling him, perched on his thighs and giving him that hot, hungry look from behind the wild mess of blond hair that shadowed her face.

He stroked his hands up her thighs, gripped her hips and pressed the aching bulge of his erection right up against the soft cotton that covered her mound in a slow, pulsing rhythm. Watching her eyes, synchronizing with her breath. Looking straight into her soul.

She cupped his face and kissed him as she moved against him.

Eventually, she moved faster, writhing eagerly, gasping for breath as she sought out the beckoning climax.

She flung her head back with a choked cry when it hit her. He held on to her, feeling the pleasure wrack her body in long, rippling shudders of pure sensation.

Afterward, she collapsed over him and hid her face against his shoulder for a long time. Catching her breath. Her body still vibrated with a high-frequency tremor.

"You good?" he asked gently.

Ava let out a soft, whispery laugh but didn't lift her face. "Oh, God," she whispered. "Yes. No. I'm destroyed. And it was amazing."

He pondered that for a moment. "Wow. Confusing. Talk about mixed messages."

"It's just so different with you," she murmured.

"Different how? Different from what?"

Ava lifted her head. "You just get so close," she said. "I know that sounds strange, but I've never felt anyone this close to me. It's like you're inside my head, and it all feels so raw. Stripped live wires. Too much power. I'm afraid I'll get fried."

He went still. "Was it too much?"

She smiled down at him. Her eyes glittered with tears. "Of course, but it's worth it," she whispered. "I didn't know it could feel like that. Like a supernova."

"I see," he said. "Supernova. Yeah. I'd call that a step in the right direction."

Ava giggled silently. "You are a master of understatement."

He lifted her up, shifting her on his lap. "Let's go for another one," he said. "I like the supernova thing. But first..."

He tugged at the bottom of her shirt. Ava let out a soft laugh and peeled it up over her head, giving him a mind-altering view of her gorgeous torso, stretching, arching, stripping. Shaking out her tousled hair. Giving him that teasing, seductive smile.

Oh, man. So beautiful. Every last damn detail. It was just killing him. His breath was ragged, too, and he lifted her up, impressed his mouth to the perfect, soft curves of her breasts. Delicious, fragrant. Smooth skin, smelling like spring flowers, and the tight bud of her nipple against his lips, his tongue, the delicate tug of his teeth.

She shivered and moaned as he loved on her gorgeous breasts, as if he was drawing pleasure from them for both of them. Because he was. He teased her nipple with his tongue as he stroked those slick, tender, secret folds between her legs, slipping inside to pet and stroke. Deliciously wet and soft. She moved helplessly against his hand.

He was so turned on, he could hardly breathe, but he sensed that she was almost there. She moved against his hand, clenching, clutching his head to her chest, her breath ragged. Those gasping whimpers. He had to see this through for her.

He could keep that going all night. An unbroken string of orgasms. Oh, yeah. He was strung out on sexy supernovas already.

Her pleasure crested and broke. He rode it out with her as she came right around his hand, gasping with sobs of pleasure. Those clutching pulses, squeezing him.

By some miracle of self-control, he held back from coming himself.

He was saving that for later.

Eight

Ava could taste the salt sweat on his muscular shoulder. Hot, intoxicating. She could lick him all over.

Something about this man moved her. Shook her. There was an endlessness to it. A sense of mortal danger, as if she were looking over a cliff so high, she couldn't see the bottom of the chasm.

Zack looked wary. "Good?" he asked again.

She nodded, and Zack set her gently on her feet and jerked the bedcover down.

He tugged her boy shorts down over her legs and tossed them away, running his hands over her bare hips with a groan of appreciation. "I can't believe how gorgeous you are," he said. "It takes my breath away."

Damn. She had to get over this goofy girlish act and start making some moves of her own, like a participating adult, but she felt so bashful and vulnerable.

But it was definitely time for him to be naked, too. She slid his athletic pants down, but the elastic waistline got hung up on his magnificent erection, so Zack reached into his pants, shifting himself around. He let the pants fall.

Oh, yeah. His bare body was just what she'd expected after writhing all over him in the pool and all that eager, exploratory petting. But that was one thick, enthusiastic erection to play with. Good thing he was wickedly good at making her wet and desperate for him. As it was, the very sight of him made her thighs clench in breathless eagerness.

He gasped at her strong grip, her slow, twisting strokes on his stiff penis. He was stone-hard, but covered with luscious velvet. Suede-smooth. Incredibly hot. Pulsing.

"You're so beautiful," she whispered.

"Glad you like it." His voice was strangled. "Please, slow down. I'm so turned on. I'm on a hair trigger right now, and I want to save it for when I'm inside you."

She squeezed his thick, solid shaft, feeling his heart throb heavily against her palm.

"It's really hard to stop," she whispered. "I love touching you."

He kissed her again, and his sensual onslaught overwhelmed her senses with pleasure and arousal. He shifted on the bed and tumbled her down on top of him.

Ava straddled him, returning his kiss with wild abandon. Stroking her own intimate flesh slowly, teasingly over the long, heavy shaft that lay against his belly. She shook with excitement as he positioned her above him, up on her knees to give him the space he needed to grip himself and caress her with the tip of his blunt phallus.

Each slow, wet, teasing, swirling stroke a sweet lash of delight.

Finally, he nudged inside, and she sank down onto him with a gasp, filled up.

Wow. She could barely move for a moment, or breathe. The sensation was overwhelming. So was the look in his eyes.

Then he started to move. She started to rock on top of him, and they found the sway, the dance. The heaving perfection of each slow, gliding thrust. Her breasts bounced, her hair dangling. She took all of him inside and loved every slick stroke.

Deeper…faster…harder, and already it was happening. The shivering tension was growing, charging. Transforming into something huge and terrifying and wonderful.

Zack stopped, holding her tightly as the climax rushed through her whole being.

Ava's eyes opened, and she reached out, stroking his cheek. Bracing herself against his big chest.

"You good?" he asked.

She smiled. "You keep asking."

"I keep wondering. I need to be sure. I need it to be excellent for you. Top-tier. Peak experience. Best ever. Nothing less will do for you."

She nodded, but she felt dismantled, disassembled. Inside out. Floating on a cloud.

"You look scared," he said. "Talk to me. Please."

Ava pressed trembling lips together. "I'm fine. It's just that I'm kind of a control freak, and this thing…

well, this is the opposite of control. I just fall to pieces with you."

"But you like it? You want more?"

"Hell, yeah, I want more. I love it. Just one thing, though."

His eyes narrowed. "Yeah? Let's hear it."

"Come along with me this time," she urged. "Don't just be a spectator. I don't want to go supernova while you watch. I want you in it with me. All the way."

He looked troubled as he slowly stroked her leg from knee to hip.

"What?" she asked. "What's the worried look?"

"I'm a control freak, too," he admitted. "The stakes have never been this high for me. I've never been this turned on in my life. I'm afraid to just go for it, no holds barred."

"I can't wait to watch you," she said. "Mmm. So sexy."

"It's different for me," he said gruffly. "I'm bigger. I have to be more careful than you do. To make sure it's good for you."

"Oh, I see." She leaned over, pressing her breasts against his chest, and laid slow, hot, sensual kisses against his collarbone while squeezing him inside herself. "I'm not worried," she whispered. "I trust you. And I've got you. Let's go for it together. See what's on the other side."

Their hands clasped, then clutched in a tight, shaking grip as he surged up inside her, plunging deep. Unleashed.

So…good. Again. Again. Every heavy stroke made

her wild for the next one. The bed shook. Their breathing was ragged. Gasps, moans, whimpers.

They both felt the power bearing down. It was like a storm rolling over them, huge and terrifying and inexorable.

They met it together, souls fused. Soaring.

At some point, Zack finally managed to roll onto his side. Ava cuddled up next to him, her hand on his heart. He buried his face in her hair and moved his hands slowly down the soft skin of her back, practically hypnotizing himself with the rhythmic caress. He ran his hand down her spine, explored her ribs, settled into the curve of her waist and the swell of her hip, and then slowly made his way back up. He wanted to commit every last detail of her to memory. Tender warmth, silken texture, sweet smell.

Then his stomach rumbled, reminding him of more mundane issues.

"Oh, hey," he said. "When I came over to knock on your door, I was going to suggest that we order dinner from room service. Are you hungry?"

"Mmm. I could probably eat something now. Do they still serve at this hour?"

"They have a reduced after-hours menu," he said. "I was checking it out before I went down to the pool."

Ava pulled loose of his embrace. "I'll go look." She laughed at the bereft expression on his face. "Come on. One of us had to get out of bed to make this happen."

"I wasn't ready," he complained. "It was way too abrupt. Traumatizing."

"Poor baby. I'll be right back." Ava went to the desk

and sorted through the hotel brochures. She picked out a menu, tossing her hair back, her sexy silhouette backlit by the light filtering out of the open bathroom door.

"The after-hours menu is short, but there are possibilities," she said. "A charcuterie board for two, with smoked Parma ham, sausage, capocollo, assorted cheeses, three types of olives and fresh fruit, and hot, crusty artisan bread. There's also a savory pastry platter. Tarts made with ricotta and zucchini flower, wild mushroom and feta, fresh asparagus and caramelized onion, and sun-dried tomatoes and goat cheese. Anything appeal to you?"

"Both of them," he said. "With a bottle of good red."

He admired her back view as she called down for room service. After a few minutes of being tormented by the visual stimulation, he got up and went closer to her, burying his face in her hair and sliding his hands over her hips as she finished ordering.

"...yes, please," she said into the phone. "And a bottle of red wine. Something that pairs well with the cheese... Yes, that sounds lovely. The sooner it's here, the happier we'll be. Yes, absolutely. Have a nice evening."

Ava put down the phone and spun around, looping her arms around his waist, and gave him that brazen temptress look that made his whole body hum. Her tousled hair cast sexy, mysterious shadows over her face, but her eyes were smiling. "So I just ordered us a picnic at one in the morning. How depraved. Oh, no. Don't you give me that look, Zack."

"What look?" he asked innocently.

"The scorching, sex-all-the-time look. No way are

we getting it on again when I've just ordered food to be brought up."

"It's a great way to distract us from our hunger while we wait," he pointed out.

"And it's a foregone conclusion that if we do get busy, they will knock on the door at the worst possible moment. I would hate that. So stop smoldering at me."

"Come on. If you're going to stand there naked, I'm going to stare at you with my jaw on the ground. You're the most beautiful woman I've ever seen. Deal with it."

"Wow," Ava murmured. "Bold words."

"True words," he said forcefully.

Her eyes dropped. "Well, then. I'll make it easier for you by jumping into the bathroom to wash up before we eat."

"Need help? I could be your bath attendant. I'll soap you up and then use the detachable showerhead to slowly, carefully rinse every single inch of you."

"Not a chance," she said, laughing. "You stay out here and be good. Listen for room service. I don't want to miss out on our dinner."

She disappeared into the bathroom, so Zack pulled on his sweatpants and went into the adjoining room to grab the terry-cloth robe. When he came back in, the hiss of water in the bathroom made sexy images form in his mind—Ava naked, hot water streaming over her perfect body. Beading on the tight tips of her breasts. Rushing over her gorgeous dips and curves to converge at the puffy little dark blond swirl of ringlets on her mound. That got him all worked up, just in time for the knock on the door. Their meal had arrived.

Zack opened the door and let the waiter push the rolling cart into the room. The guy left with a big smile on his face when Zack pushed the tip into his hand.

He tapped on the bathroom door. "Food's here," he called out.

"Be right out!" she called back.

Ava emerged from the bathroom, pulling the tie that had held up her hair up and letting it tumble luxuriously over her shoulders. He had the wine poured and the food laid out. She accepted the goblet from him and sipped it with a smile. "Oh, that's nice."

"It is," he agreed. "The food looks great. And the pastries are hot, so let's get to it."

The food was incredible. As if being with Ava had sharpened his senses. The bread was chewy and flavorful, and the tarts were delicious, the crusts flaky and buttery. Thin-sliced salt-cured ham was melt-in-your-mouth tender. The cheeses exploded with flavor. There were bowls of fat, shiny Greek and Italian olives, big aromatic green grapes, sliced black figs and fat golden pears to finish. Everything tasted freaking perfect.

They polished off all of it, leaving just crumbs, pits, grape stems and pear cores.

Ava looked oddly shy in the silence that followed. Her cheeks were very red.

"Damn," he said. "This hotel gets points for kick-ass midnight feast capability. Usually, it's a club sandwich if you're lucky and a frozen pizza if you're not. Only one thing missing. Dessert."

"I didn't even think of it," Ava said. "Shall we look at the menu again? We can see if they have anything that's—"

"I had a different treat in mind."

Her eyes widened as he stood up, circling the table in two strides, and knelt down in front of her, then gently tugged and spun her in the chair so that she sat facing him.

The movement made the terry-cloth robe fall wider open over her perfect thighs, and gave him a teasing glimpse of that shadowy perfection between them. He stroked his hands slowly over her warm skin, all the way up to her hips, feeling her shiver in response.

He bent down to kiss the soft skin over her knees. "I don't need the menu," he told her. "Everything I want is right here." He worked his way up her thigh with slow, languid, lazy kisses. No hurry. He'd get to the gates of paradise soon enough.

Ava covered her face, laughing under her breath. "I don't know what my problem is," she whispered. "It's ridiculous to be embarrassed after what we just did. You have such a strange effect on me, Zack. You make me all bashful and fluttery."

"I hope that's not a bad thing."

She dropped her hands, smiling at him. "Not bad," she assured him. "Just super-intense. Every sensation is amplified. The stakes feel so much higher."

Yeah, she had it exactly right. The stakes were higher. Infinitely high. But he didn't want to discuss that right now, not with his mouth watering for her intoxicating taste. So he just kissed his way slowly up her thighs, letting his hands slide into the velvety warmth of her secret places. Exploring the dips and swells and sensitive places. Caressing her tender folds. Hot, sweet, softer than a cloud. So perfect. Probing, petting. Coaxing.

Finally, he felt that ripple and sigh of total surrender

go through her, and her legs relaxed. He gently pushed them open and tugged her forward to the edge of her chair, pressing his face to her belly. Her slender fingers held his head, stroking his short hair.

She let out a choked gasp as he put his mouth to her. "Oh, Zack."

So damn good. Her taste, her texture. It blasted off fireworks in his mind, his body. Even so, some part of him was hyperaware of how fine a line he was walking right now. He hadn't understood the danger of the Ava paradox, not before being so deep inside her. Moving in her, melded with her, like he'd always fantasized about.

But getting what he wanted so badly had not satisfied him. This craving was insatiable.

When it came to Ava, the more he feasted, the hungrier he got.

Nine

Mom's eyes were full of fear as she clutched both Ava's hands and stared into her eyes. Her mouth moved and she was yelling something urgent, but there was too much noise to make out the words. Black smoke filled the plane cabin, sparks, flames. Things flew past them. All she heard was panicked screaming and the roar of wind in their ears as the plane was torn apart in the sky—

Her hands were ripped from Mom's and she was alone, spinning through empty space. The ground below rose to meet her, faster and faster—

Ava jolted awake with a gasp. Choking off the shriek of terror just in time.

Her heart was pounding. Her body shook violently. Zack stirred, and his arms tightened around her. "Av? You okay?" he murmured.

She twisted away and sat up, letting her hair fall forward to curtain her face. Gasping for breath, but trying to do it quietly. She didn't want him to see her face, even in the dim half-light from the bathroom. "Sure," she forced out, breathless. "Fine."

But he was on to her now. He lifted himself up onto his elbow, putting his hand on her back. "Are you?" he asked. "You don't seem fine. Bad dream?"

She jerked away from his touch, still shivering. "I'm fine," she repeated.

She slid off the bed and hurried to the bathroom, fighting tears and the cold, sucking emptiness behind them. It was pulling her down. Dragging her under.

Even now, even tonight, after the absolute best sex she'd ever had or even imagined having, with the man she'd always wanted. Even now, here she was again, in her usual dark pit. It had been childish and stupid to hope that just the magic of getting thoroughly and magnificently laid would suddenly fix all her problems for her.

That was too much to ask of a roll in the hay. Even a spectacular one.

She twisted up her hair, set the shower running and stepped inside. It was easier to cry if her face was already wet, and crying gave relief sometimes. She didn't know what to do with Zack. She couldn't manage him and her dark pit at the same time, with all his charisma and his potent emotional charge. He wanted so much from her.

She would disintegrate from the pressure.

She wasn't really surprised. She'd felt that desperate

intensity the last time they made love, as the morning drew closer. As if they were trying to outrun something.

Yeah, right. That was because she was. But in the end, it always took her down.

A memory from her high school physics class flitted across her mind. Newton's third law of motion. *For every action there is an equal and opposite reaction.* One of the few physics facts that had stuck with her. But Newton's third law had lingered in her mind because it made emotional sense to her. It rang in her mind like a bell.

This fear, clawing inside her. This was the equal and opposite reaction. The price that had to be paid for anything that wonderful. Nothing came for free.

She took her time once she finished with her shower, styling her hair, putting moisturizer on her face. Hoping the feelings would subside if she focused completely on something else. Anything else. Sometimes it worked. For a while.

No such luck today, though. She dabbed a little concealer under her reddened eyes.

Her face was pale, but not her lips. They were hot red, and a little swollen, from hours of desperate, frantic kissing. Just thinking about it sent the sense memories pulsing through her body, making her thighs clench and her breath catch in her chest.

Stop stalling. Just do this. It has to be done.

She put in her gold and ruby earrings, pulled on the terry-cloth bathrobe and marched out into the room.

Zack was sitting up in bed, waiting for her. Her gaze locked with his for an unbearable instant and skittered away as if she'd touched a raw current of electricity. She got to work laying out clothes for the day. Underwear, stockings, skirt, blouse, coat, boots.

"Ava," he said. "Please. Just tell me. What's wrong? What did I do?"

"Nothing. Really, nothing," she said, because it was the simple truth. He was wonderful. That was what made this so awful. The unfairness of it. What a goddamn waste, that she couldn't let herself enjoy this as it should be enjoyed.

But she just couldn't. She was too raw. Too wrecked.

Zack studied her as she pulled her underwear on and hooked her bra, a frown of focused concentration in his eyes. "Bullshit," he said. "Tell me. Please."

She sat down on the other bed to pull her stockings on. "Really. It's nothing. Just this time of day. I'm at a really low ebb. Not a morning person. No fun to be with."

"Don't put your clothes on yet," he said. "It's early. I could make you forget what time of day it is if you gave me a chance. That's a challenge I'm willing to embrace."

She tugged her stockings up and slipped on her blouse. "No," she said tightly. "I, um…sorry, Zack, but I actually could use a little privacy right now."

Zack's face stiffened. He slid out of bed and picked up his sweatpants, pulling them on. "Okay. I get it."

"You—you don't. Really. It doesn't have anything to do with you," she told him swiftly. "It's just me. My own weird issues. Please don't take it personally."

He let out a bitter laugh. "Sorry, but that's not an option right now," he said. "This whole thing has gotten pretty damn personal for me. So don't even try."

"I didn't mean to—"

"I don't care what you meant or didn't mean. I'll get

out of your way while you dress, but don't leave the room without me. I still want you covered at all times." He stopped by the door, careful not to meet her eyes. "It'll take me maybe ten minutes to grab a shower, get shaved and dressed. I'll be waiting for your knock."

"All right, but Zack, please don't get upset," she begged.

"How could I not? After what happened last night, the way you're acting sucks for me. You can't talk it away."

"I didn't mean to make you feel—"

"Too bad. It happened anyway. You think you're the only one with feelings? The rest of us should just suck it up? Play it cool so that you won't be inconvenienced?"

"No," she said miserably. "I don't think that at all."

Zack shook his head. "Get ready for your day, Ava." His voice was colorless. "Don't sweat it. I don't want to embarrass you or make things complicated. We're adults. It's fine. Take it easy."

The door closed. She fell forward onto the bed and buried her face in the pillow. It still smelled of him. Keeping her scream silent hurt. Like a screw turning in her throat.

She'd struck out in love before. Often. But it had been different the other times. Her past lovers had just backed away when things got difficult. Sometimes she'd even felt a sense of numb relief when they were gone. One less thing to stress about.

Not this time.

Zack scanned the stream of people cycling through the Blooms' trade show booth, which was packed and buzzing with activity. Apparently, Desert Bloom was the hottest prospect of Future Innovation. The food and drinks being served created a party atmosphere, with tray after tray of fresh-baked, artisanal crackers smeared with olive, artichoke or sun-dried tomato paste continually brought in by the catering crew, all treats prepared exclusively with Desert Bloom Farm products. Visitors devoured them as fast as they were delivered and kept Ernest busy pouring out Desert Bloom wines and mojitos.

Ava had not looked Zack's way once all morning and into the afternoon. Not that she'd had time. She was busy being whatever the situation required her to be, on the spot. Marketer, storyteller, branding specialist, crisis manager, cheerleader, shrink. She never strayed from the Blooms, who looked hunched and spiderlike in their black turtleneck sweaters and jeans, but they were relatively well-groomed today, having attempted to tame their bushy clouds of hair. They were wound up so tight, they tended to babble, so Ava was always at their elbows, nudging the conversation where it needed to go, but she did it so expertly, only someone watching as closely as he was would ever notice.

At least in this context, no one could call his intense, focused attention creepy. It was his goddamn job to hover over her, staring like a madman. Lucky for him.

He'd been such an idiot, getting his poor, tender feelings all hurt this morning. But the real idiocy was in giving in to temptation in the first place. What the hell did he expect from her? Birds and flowers and true love, after one night? It was just great sex. Any other guy with a brain would have been more than happy to settle for that, at face value.

But not him. Oh, no. He just had to make it as hard as possible for himself.

Wanting more. Wanting it all. Wanting it right freaking *now*.

On some level, he'd known he would crash and burn if he gave in to this urge. He'd known it for years, but a man could only hold out for so long. Ava Maddox, dripping wet, in a bikini, her gorgeous blue eyes hot with desire...how could he resist that?

He couldn't. And now he was paying for his lustful stupidity.

Craig Redding happened to be in the large group of men that were clustered around her, which did not thrill him. The guy was handsy as all hell. He kept touching Ava's shoulder, her arm, her back, her hair. Throwing a possessive arm over her shoulder. There he was, doing it again, even after she slipped his grip. At one point, he even pinched her cheek. Ava jerked away and wagged a warning finger at him, laughing. Too bad there was no pool here for her to dunk the presumptuous bonehead. Just as well, though, since Zack would be tempted to hold that entitled jerk's head underwater until he stopped flopping.

A raucous burst of laughter from the direction of the bar caught his attention.

It was Ernest, at the bar. He was giggling, his head together with another young guy. Tall, skinny, with straight black hair.

Ernest saw Zack look over and lifted the pitcher of

mojito that he'd freshly replenished from the chilled urn behind him. "We're celebrating. You want some?"

"What's the occasion?" Zack asked.

Ernest beckoned him to come closer and leaned to whisper in his ear, his breath heavy with alcohol. "See that guy who's talking to Ava?" Ernest whispered. "Brown coat, balding, ears sticking out like jug handles? That's Trevor Wexford."

Ernest saw Zack's expression and nodded. "I see you've heard the name?"

"Big venture capitalist, right?" Zack said.

"Duh," Ernest said. "Like, huge. And that's his wife next to him, Callista. She's a real piece of work. The two of them have been here talking to Ava and the Blooms for over forty minutes. He's taken all their literature and given her his card. He's interested. Which is huge." Ernest dragged over the big pitcher and hoisted it up, slopping some of the liquid onto the bar. "Want a mojito? Sustainably farmed sugar and rum, lemons and fresh mint from the Desert Bloom farm. Or wine, from the organic Desert Bloom vineyard?"

The two young men dissolved into drunken giggles once again. Zack studied them for a moment. "Looks like the two of you have done some quality control already."

"Um, well." Ernest's new friend smirked. "Someone had to do it, right?"

"Who are you?" Zack asked.

"Oh, sorry," Ernest said. "I should have introduced you. This is Malik. He's Craig Redding's assistant."

"Ah. I see," Zack said.

"So can I pour you a drink?" Ernest asked. "Or some wine? The wine's good, too."

"I'm on the job," Zack told him.

Ernest tittered. "No problem. I've got you covered, along with all the other teetotalers." He pulled another big pitcher from the shelf behind him. "Here's your no-alcohol option, a virgin Desert Bloom. Basically, it's just a glass of really fabulous minty lemonade." Ernest poured out a cup and presented it to Zack. "The cups are sustainable, too. Made from leaves, each one stamped with a flower from the Desert Bloom garden. Same with the plates. Ava's branding idea."

Zack took the cup and admired the stamped dried flower that adorned the delicate veined surface of the leaf. "Nice design."

"Yeah, and one hundred percent compostable," Ernest told him. "And I'm the lucky guy who gets to load up the biodegradable garbage bags full of all the plates and cups and drag them out to the truck to haul back to the Desert Bloom compost center. Gotta be flex in this brave new world, right? I'm not just a marketer now. I'm also a janitor, garbage man, busboy, waiter and bartender! All the things! Wow, lucky me!"

Zack waited until Ernest and Malik got through their fresh snorting fit of laughter before he replied. "Your boss is over there working a whole lot more jobs than you are," he said. "I don't see her bitching and moaning about it. Or drinking, either."

Ernest and Malik abruptly swallowed their laughter, exchanging nervous glances.

Zack went on. "Seems to me that a big, important trade show where a lot is at stake for your employer isn't the best venue for you to get hammered with your buddy." He looked at Malik. "And I'm guessing that your boss would agree with me. Am I right?"

Malik's eyes slid away. "Uh…uh…dude," he muttered to Ernest. "I better go and, uh, check on some stuff. Catch up with you later."

Malik vanished, and Ernest just stood there for a moment, red-faced. "You don't have to get all moralistic about it, you know," he said. "It's not like I'm sloshed. Just a tiny buzz. I had barely a taste of the mojitos. I'm totally on top of my game."

"Good," Zack said. "Stay there. It's what she pays you for." He took a sip of his virgin Desert Bloom mojito. "Good stuff. Very minty. My compliments."

"I'm going to get another case of lemons," Ernest said, slinking away.

Zack drained his compostable cup of virgin mojito and tossed it into the receptacle provided, then shifted his position to get Ava back into his unbroken line of vision. She was still chatting with the guy Ernest had identified as Trevor Wexford. His wife and Ava were laughing at something he'd said.

"Hey, there, Zackie! Wasn't that your first name?"

Zack turned at the sound of that oily voice to see Craig Redding shoving a cracker smeared with artichoke paste into his mouth. The guy smiled at him as he chewed and washed it all down with a big gulp of mojito.

"The name is Zack," he said.

"Right," Craig said. "Chief security officer at Maddox Hill, eh? Quite a job. Huge company. Thousands of far-flung workers all over the globe. A crap ton of priceless intellectual property to protect. I'm surprised to see you straying so far from your flock."

"I've got an excellent team," Zack told him. "I have complete confidence in them to manage for a few days without me."

"That's nice to hear," Craig said. "A high-functioning workplace is a thing of beauty, right?"

"Absolutely," Zack said.

"I guess you'd know," Craig said. "You've been in the game at every level. From the very bottom on up. Right?"

Zack crossed his arms and studied the other man. "I suppose," he said. "Where exactly are you going with this?"

"Not anywhere in particular," Craig said, his voice elaborately casual. "I read a profile on you in the *C-Suite* magazine."

"Oh, yeah. They did one a couple years ago," Zack said.

"Yeah. I remember reading it a while back," Craig said. "Nice article. The writer must have had a crush on you. They just went on and on."

Huh. Craig had stalked him online, reading archived articles. That was weird.

"I'm gratified at your interest," he said guardedly. "I just don't get the point of it."

"I take an interest in the arcs of people's careers," Craig said. "You started out as a bodyguard back in the day, right? An army buddy of Drew Maddox, current CEO. The founder's nephew. He got you a job doing close protection for Hendrick Hill when he traveled to Africa after you got out of the army. Am I right?"

"Not exactly," Zack said. "It was the marines, not the army. And yes, Drew suggested that I apply for the job, but he didn't hand it to me. He wasn't even working at Maddox Hill back then. He was still in architecture school."

"Yeah, yeah, right. So it was all on your own merit, of course. Quite the success story. Real inspiring. Rags to riches, huh?"

Zack gazed at Redding, thinking about his single mom, a small-town social worker, and how she'd worked two jobs, scraping and scrambling to make sure he and Joanna had decent clothes.

"I wouldn't exactly say rags," he replied.

"You wouldn't? Huh. Guess everything's relative, right?" Craig's exposed teeth had a stringy wad of sustainably farmed Desert Bloom garden mint stuck between them.

"Guess so," Zack agreed.

"So this thing with Ava," Craig pressed on. "It's a career flashback? You're, what...devolving, professionally? Regressing? How should I call it?"

"Call it doing a favor for a friend," Zack said. "Then go about your business."

Craig's eyes narrowed. "That was rude and hostile. Fighting words, eh?"

"Not at all," Zack said. "I don't need to fight you. I'm just saving you time and energy. This conversation serves no purpose. Go talk to someone who cares."

Craig's nostrils flared, but he turned around and walked away, right back to Ava. He bent down and murmured in her ear. Probably something about Zack's fighting words. Running to tattle on him, like the whining, gutless twerp that he was.

Ava flashed Zack a startled look. *Ooh, busted.* He held his breath, wondering if she was going to come over and scold him for being such a bad, rude boy.

She turned away. Nope, no such luck. That brief, fleeting glance was all he got.

She was just so damn beautiful. Even if it hadn't literally been his job to keep his eyes glued to her, he wouldn't have been able to do anything else. And he wasn't the only one. Every man in her orbit rubbernecked. And he didn't blame them one goddamn bit.

However, if a rubbernecker happened to catch Zack's eye, he whipped his gaze away from Ava instantly and marched right onward without stopping to look at the Blooms' booth. That was Zack's small personal superpower. Silent intimidation.

Or so he had been told.

Using it like this displayed a distinct lack of professionalism on his part, but that was just too damn bad. God knew, the booth got plenty of cracker-chomping, mojito-guzzling traffic anyway.

He was doing them a favor by helping them sort out the wheat from the chaff.

The man just wiped her out. No matter where she went or whom she talked to, Zack was there, blasting out a frequency so intense, it exhausted her.

When she wrapped things up on the expo floor and said good night to the Blooms, she went to the bar to meet some old friends for a late drink. She'd known Marcus and Caleb Moss, the CTO and CEO of Moss-

Tech, for years. Caleb had been one of her first clients in the way back, when he'd opened a start-up tech business with a friend of his years ago. Sadly, the start-up had ended in catastrophe, through no fault of hers or Caleb's. But they had remained friends since then, and they'd made plans that morning to talk about the MossTech expo project, which was on the short list of candidates for the Future Innovation prize, along with the Blooms'.

Nothing would persuade Zack to leave her alone for a drink with her friends in the hotel bar. His only concession was to sit on the other side of the bar, with clear sight lines, and watch them all stonily from afar while nursing a club soda with lime.

Stoic, expressionless and unnerving as hell.

It didn't help that the Moss brothers were both extremely good-looking. No doubt that jacked up Zack's hellfire-and-brimstone stare an extra couple of notches in intensity.

Marcus and Caleb's conversation kept trailing off to nothing as they shot quick, unsettled glances in Zack's direction.

"Ava," Caleb said cautiously. "In the interests of personal safety, what's the deal with the guy fixated on you from across the bar? Is there something we should know?"

Ava rubbed her forehead with a sigh. "Some interpersonal conflict," she said, her voice weary. "Nothing to do with you. I imagine you heard about my problem with online trolls, right?"

"Yes," Marcus said. "Bottom-feeding scum. I hope you crush whoever it is."

"Yeah, thanks. Anyhow, it kind of blew up this week, so I went to Zack for advice. He's Maddox Hill's CSO, and he got all twisted up and upset about it. He insisted on coming down from Seattle to keep an eye on me down here, but somehow it's gotten really, ah…complicated."

"Yeah, no kidding," Caleb said.

"Do us a favor, babe," Marcus said. "Just make sure he knows that the two of us don't have designs on you, okay? Stunning though you are, you've never given either one of us a break, and at this point, I have no reason to think you ever will. And it's a sure thing we aren't going to try any funny stuff with that big, scary dude looming over you."

She swatted him on the shoulder. "Oh, shut up. I'm not involved with him."

Caleb and Marcus exchanged dubious glances. "I wouldn't want to be the one to tell him that," Caleb said.

Ava fought back a startling wave of tears, but she did not want to inflict that embarrassment on her friends. "There's attraction, yes," she admitted, her voice tight. "Big-time. But we just hit a wall, and it's better to stop now. Before we hurt ourselves."

Marcus studied her face. "I think that ship has sailed, Av. For him, anyway."

Her gaze dropped, and she bit her lip to keep it steady.

"Right," Marcus said. "Just as I thought. That ship already sailed for you, too."

"I'm sorry, Av," Caleb said awkwardly. "That sucks."

"Oh, stop it, guys," she snapped. "Enough already. I came here to talk about your plant DNA diagnostic techniques, not my love life. Moving on. You should consider having MossTech partner with Bobby and Wilbur. Your research could really complement theirs. I want to set up a meeting sometime."

She turned the conversation to business, and the Mosses played along. They discussed DNA diagnostics at some length. Finally, she gave them both a peck on the cheek and promised to visit their booth the next day.

Zack materialized beside her as she walked to the elevator.

"Zack, for God's sake," she whispered. "Would you just stop?"

"Doing what? My job? No, I won't stop."

"That's not what I meant, and you know it. I'm referring to the glaring and the scolding and the general negativity. It's embarrassing. You got Ernest all upset—"

"He needed his ass kicked. He got sloppy today."

"Maybe so, but that's my problem, not yours. I'm the one who pays him. And that thing you said to Craig was just rude and ridiculous. I know he's annoying, but seriously?"

"I didn't like the way he was sliming you," Zack said. "He was bugging me."

She blew out a breath through her teeth. "You are making problems for me, Zack."

"Sorry. I should have gotten someone else to come down here to replace me, but this event wraps up soon. Once we're back in Seattle, Vikram's team will cover you and I'll monitor the situation from a distance. You'll never have to see my face again."

She stopped in front of her door. “Goddammit, Zack,” she whispered. “This is just unbearable.”

“It’ll be over soon,” he said. “Grit your teeth.”

The stony quality in his voice made her as angry as she was miserable. “I never let people bug me,” she said. “Living with Uncle Malcolm gave me a very thick skin, and I’m good at letting things roll off my back. But you just drive me totally nuts.”

The look on his face was more like a brick wall than ever before. He wasn’t going to risk letting her hurt him again. And she didn’t blame him after the way she’d panicked this morning. Like she always did when the tide went out and left her sick and stranded.

No, this raw voltage was just too dangerous. They scared each other to death.

“If you need to swim tonight, let me know,” he said.

“God, no,” she said. “I’m exhausted.”

“Then I’ll let you rest. Good night.” He stood there waiting until she swiped her key card and the light clicked green.

“Good night,” she whispered.

Ava dropped her purse on the table and sank down onto the bed. Some part of her was always listening for sounds of Zack in the other room. She wondered if he would order dinner. Her eyes fell on the room service menu, the wine list. The memories of last night burned in her mind. The longing to reach out to him was physically painful.

But any attempt to make this better would definitely only make it worse.

Zack was not the kind of guy one could dally with

and then send back to his room when she was done. If Zack did something at all, he did it all the way.

And all night long, with devastating, tireless energy and skill.

And when he was angry, oh God. The whole world felt it.

Ten

Twenty-five hours to go.

Zack ran that through his mind. He heard Ava's easy laughter while she chatted with the people outside the booth. She looked as stunning as ever in a tailored dark pantsuit and an ice-blue silk blouse.

Then a flash of coral pink caught his eye. He turned to see Callista Wexford enter the exhibition booth and approach Bobby and Wilbur, who were bent over a glass case full of flowering plants. Callista flashed them a brilliant smile and tossed her mane of glossy mahogany hair back. "Excuse me, gentlemen. I've noticed that fungi appear to be the mainstay of your seed conditioner potion. More so than the other microbes in your inoculation brew, which makes it different from some of the other projects of this kind that I've reviewed. Why this focus on the fungi?"

Callista waited expectantly, but her smile seemed to freeze in place as the Bloom brothers just stared back, eyes blank, mouths agape.

Damn. They were glitching. Their circuits were just not built to handle the massive charge of Callista's feminine splendor. She'd flash-fried them.

Zack racked his brains to remember everything he'd learned in the past day as he stepped forward. "I think the issue is to reduce the soil's exposure to erosive force," he offered. "The fungi stabilize the soil by making it into sticky lumps, which makes it more resistant to erosion. Did I get that more or less right, Wilbur?"

Wilbur blinked as his brain stuttered back online, his eyes darting between Zack and Callista. "Uh…uh…yes," he stammered. "It's, uh…glomalin. The soil particles form water-stable aggregates, and root entanglements, fungal hyphae and exudates pull it all together and help the soil hold water and resist erosion."

"But we haven't discounted rhizosphere bacteria," Bobby assured her. "Everything has its place in the process. But our focus here is to match the right fungi to the right plant to bring the soil to life as fast as possible. Which helps it hold the rain that falls on it."

And the Blooms were off and running, blasting out info about vegetation dynamics, soil stability and anionic-hydrophilic polymers. Not long after that, Callista extricated herself and joined Zack outside the booth.

"Wow," she murmured. "That was intense. Like turning on a fire hose."

"Yeah, the Blooms are really something," Zack agreed. "Great project, isn't it?"

"Oh, marvelous. So what's your role in all this?" Callista fluttered her eyelashes at him expertly. "Do you have a horse in this race?"

"Not yet, but it looks like a great investment," he said. "I just recently learned about it. I work at Maddox Hill myself. I'm just here because I accompanied Ava to the trade show."

"So you two are, ah…together?"

"I'm just here to provide security," Zack said, leaving it at that.

But Callista would not leave it where he put it. "I see. Is that why you never leave her side?"

His jaw clenched painfully. "Yes, I guess it would explain that."

Callista's smile widened. She eased closer to him. "So you're based in Seattle?"

She made a small, satisfied sound when he nodded. "Trevor and I have a place up there," she said. "We own a small island in Puget Sound, just a short boat trip from the city. Gorgeous place. Just water, birds and trees as far as the eyes can see. I spend a lot of time there. Sadly, Trevor's almost always working, so he practically never comes up with me." Callista placed her hand on his forearm. "I'm spending the next couple of weeks at the island, since I'm planning to attend the Maddox Hill Foundation gala." Her voice was throaty. "Come see me. I'll send a boat for you. Just tell me when."

Zack gazed down at the slender, perfectly manicured hand resting on his sleeve, adorned with costly rings and bracelets, and realized several surprising things all at once.

One, he wasn't into her. She was a stunner, sure.

A man would have to be dead not to notice. But he was hooked on Ava's incandescent glow. Ava's beauty seemed deeper, more vivid. Other women looked flat to him by comparison.

He didn't know what to say to Callista. He wasn't talented at fabricating convincing social lies. He tended to default to the plain truth, but in this case, the truth sounded churlish and ugly. *You're married, and I don't want to go through that particular wood chipper. I'm not intrigued by neglected trophy wives on the prowl for fresh meat.*

Or worst of all, the most stark and naked truth of all. *Sorry, but I'm all hung up someone else.* God help him.

"Oh, hey, Callista." He turned when he heard Ava's voice. She was smiling when he turned to look, but with none of her usual warmth. "See something that you like?"

"Oh, yes," Callista purred. "Most definitely."

The women's brilliant smiles were like blades clashing. "Wilbur and Bobby were just telling Callista about soil stabilization via inoculation with AM fungi," Zack said, just to break the tension.

"Yes, they told me a lot of things, very quickly," Callista said, tittering. "But Zack's simple explanation about sticky dirt clumps really made it pop for me. Zack is an excellent brand ambassador. You should hire him to make the science digestible for us normal folk."

"He'd be far too expensive," Ava said crisply. "He's a busy man. A chief executive at Maddox Hill Architecture. No time for side hustles or science projects."

"No? Like, say, doing close protection work for you?" Callista blinked at her innocently.

"That's a special case," Zack said.

"I am sure that it is," Callista murmured. "Very special." She fished a card from her small purse and tucked it into his suit pocket. "If you feel like talking about that thing we discussed, or if you decide to carve out time for a side hustle, call me. Later, Ava. Be sure to tell Wilbur and Bobby that Trevor and I are rooting for them tonight."

"Certainly I will. Thanks," Ava said.

Her smile vanished as soon as Callista turned the corner. Ava turned toward Zack.

She finally broke the odd silence. "So what did you discuss with Callista?" Her voice was casual, but her eyes were anything but.

"Nothing in particular," Zack hedged. "She asked Bobby and Wilbur about arbuscular mycorrhizal fungi, and they both froze up. Either her cleavage or her perfume, or both. I primed the pump for them, got them talking, and after that, they were fine. And lucky for me, because I put out everything I had."

"Oh, I just bet you did," Ava said.

The hackles rose on Zack's neck. "Excuse me? What is that supposed to mean?"

"Oh, nothing," she said, her voice light. "I really appreciate you pulling Wilbur and Bobby back on track. I should have been covering them myself. They aren't equipped to function with a woman like Callista Wexford." She paused for a moment. "And I hope you'll forgive me for saying this, but I don't think you are, either."

Zack gaped at her. "Where the hell did that come from?"

"I know, I know," Ava said. "You're a free man. Do

anything you want with that card in your pocket. But I've known Callista for years. She'll stomp right on your face to get what she wants. Keep that in mind before you wander into her sticky web."

"I have no intention of wandering into anybody's sticky web," he growled. "The warning isn't necessary. Or appropriate."

"So sorry. My bad," she murmured, looking unrepentant. "Oh, hey. Looks like they're calling me back out there. Excuse me." She slipped away.

He set off to follow her, keeping his eyes fixed on that honey-colored updo as it bobbed through the throng. She stopped at a group of Bobby and Wilbur's best prospects. Trevor Wexford and Craig Redding were in the group.

Zack forced his way closer, and Craig spotted him. Zack saw a contemptuous smile flit across his face, and before Zack could close the distance, Ava stumbled and fought for balance as Craig grabbed her arm and pulled her in the opposite direction. The *hell*?

Zack pushed through the crowd as fast as he could without knocking people over. He followed Craig and Ava into an adjoining room, filled with tables, not as crowded as the expo floor. Craig pulled her into a quieter corner and turned in mock surprise as Zack approached. "Well, if it isn't Zackie the guard dog, sniffing along behind."

"Let go of her," Zack said.

Ava turned her head with a gasp, her eyes wide. "Zack, please don't—"

"Don't overreact, pal." Craig raised both hands, smirking. "Keep it mellow."

"Step away from her, right now."

"Zack!" Ava's eyes were horrified. "Calm down! I've known Craig for ten years. We went to school together. He's not a danger to me. Relax!"

"Yeah, Zack," Craig taunted. "Relax. She's safe. We're just going to get lunch."

"She's not going anywhere without a bodyguard," Zack said.

"You've got to be kidding." Craig gave Ava a disbelieving glance, then looked back at Zack. "Rest easy, buddy. We're grabbing lunch to talk about old times and future opportunities. She'll be fine. What could possibly happen?"

"We'll never find out," Zack said. "I'm not leaving her, with you or anyone."

"And this stupid power struggle is beside the point!" Ava interjected. "I don't have time for lunch with you, Craig, as I already told you. The brothers need me as a go-between. I'm networking! And Zack, you are out of line."

"No, I am not," Zack replied, still staring at Craig. "By no means."

"What is it with this guy?" Craig asked. "Is he your guard dog or your boyfriend?"

Ava recoiled, her mouth tightening. "That was uncalled-for, Craig. Back off."

"I get it." Craig's voice had a tone of discovery. "This poor bozo doesn't know which one he is. Eenie, meenie, miney, mo, right? Guard dog or boyfriend? You've got his pointy little jarhead all confused."

"You're pissing me off, Craig," Ava told him. "Get lost."

"Dirty girl." Craig clucked his tongue. "You should know better, Ava. Things get messy real fast when you start screwing the help."

Zack had no memory of getting there, but he was suddenly nose to nose with Craig Redding, his hand twisted into the other man's shirt collar, pinning him against the wall. Craig's feet dangled over empty air, and his face was red. His eyes bulged.

"Apologize to her, you foulmouthed son of a bitch." Zack shook the guy to get him going, but Craig just gurgled and coughed, wiggling frantically. "Let's hear it. Speak up."

From far away, he heard Ava's frantic voice, far outside the roar in his own ears. Then he noticed her hands, smacking at his shoulders and his chest, then scrabbling with her nails at his fingers, still clenched around Craig's collar.

Ava was yelling in his face. "Let him go! Damn it, Zack!"

It went against every instinct to let that trash-talking punk stand on own his feet after what he'd said to Ava. Craig was in desperate need of a pounding.

Wrong place. Wrong time. He was doing himself no favors with this floor show.

Zack exhaled slowly and dropped Craig back on his feet. He stepped back.

Craig pitched forward, almost falling, and hunched there with his hands braced on his knees, coughing and sputtering.

Ava put her hand on his shoulder. "Craig, are you all—"

"Don't touch me!" Craig flinched away from her

hand. His face was dark red with rage as he pointed at Zack. "You are a goddamn animal!"

"Better that than an asshole," Zack told him.

Craig sucked in a gasp of fresh outrage. "Leash your damned dog, Ava!"

"Just go, Craig," Ava said tightly. "Please. You've caused enough trouble."

Craig slouched out of the room, muttering.

Ava turned to him. "What in the hell was that? Never do that to me again!"

"I didn't do anything to you. I did it to him. For insulting you."

"I can fight my own battles!"

"Yeah? Then why did you come to me with your problem in the first place, if you're completely on top of it?"

"That is unfair," she said furiously. "My trolls are another issue. You are here to defend my physical safety, not my honor, and you're here at your own insistence, not mine. Craig is no threat to my physical safety! And I'm no fragile Victorian damsel with her smelling salts. I can defend my own goddamn honor!"

"He disrespected you," he said. "I can't allow that."

"It's not up to you!" Ava yelled. "I am not helpless! I can answer any disrespect that comes my way in person! I don't need a champion. Do you understand?"

Zack just gazed back at her and said nothing.

Ava's eyes widened. "Zack?" she prompted. "Hello? This is the part where you promise me that you won't do this to me again."

"I don't make promises unless I'm sure that I can keep them. If that sleazy punk insults you or gets up in my face again, I can't promise I won't break his jaw." He held up his hand as she opened her mouth. "Let me finish. He's a slimy little weasel, so I doubt it'll come to that. He doesn't have a death wish. It's a nonissue. He won't get near me."

Or you. The silent subtext.

Ava made an impatient sound. "I don't have time for your Neanderthal posturing right now. I'm going to get back to work. And you will not get in my way. Understood?"

"Absolutely," he said. "No one will get in your way. That's what I'm here for. To scare away the riffraff. That's my particular specialty."

She glared at him. "You just never stop, do you?"

"Never," he said.

Eleven

Ava didn't hear another word out of Zack for the rest of that frenetic afternoon, but she was intensely aware of his presence. He just stood there like a colossus, a few steps away from wherever she was, letting people sidle nervously around him.

His burning focus never relented, not even as she, Ernest and the Bloom brothers walked together to the elevator to prepare for the dinner and the awards ceremony. Zack paced along quietly beside them as she tried to calm down the Blooms, but three days of constant extroversion had taken its toll. Wilbur and Bobby were exhausted. Both of the brothers were pale and sweaty, with wild eyes and trembling hands.

"We'll come to your room in a half an hour," Ava reminded, patting Wilbur on the shoulder. "Take it easy. You guys will be great. I know it."

"But I can't knot a tie," Wilbur lamented. "And Bobby's even worse at it. Can I just wear a T-shirt under my suit coat? It's black, at least. I hate button-down shirts."

"Not tonight, Wilbur. Wear the shirt, please," Ava urged. "And relax. You guys just blew everybody's minds with your beautiful project. It will change the course of history. Remember, you're selling the one thing every person here or anywhere would pay any price for—hope for the future. A healthier, richer planet for our kids and grandkids. You two are the good guys, answering the call of duty to the whole world, so stand tall and own it. Chests out. Heads up. Be the guys who can make that dream a reality."

"Um…okay," Bobby said, wiping his broad, shiny forehead. "But…the ties?"

"Zack will help you knot the ties before we go down. Right, Zack?"

"Sure I will," Zack calmly assured them. "I've got your back. My granddad taught me to do it when I was ten. You guys will rock this. I'll bet you'll win that prize, too."

Ernest got off at the same floor as the Blooms and hustled them off the elevator.

"See you in a half hour," Ava called. "Wear the button-down shirt, Wilbur! And drink a glass of water, both of you!"

The elevator door closed, and she was alone with Zack Austin, which at this point made her just as jumpy and shaky as Bobby and Wilbur.

Zack gave her a thoughtful look. "You take this whole thing so personally."

"Of course I do," she replied. "How else could I take

it? Those guys are my buddies. I've known them since freshman year in college. They're like my goofy little brothers. And they need my help like no client of mine has ever needed it before."

"Really? More than Jenna? You did incredible things for Arm's Reach when you started working for her foundation."

The door slid open on their floor, and Ava considered his question as they walked together. "Not the same," she said. "Jenna is a perfectly competent brand ambassador in her own right. She just needed me to pump energy into her project, mostly to free up more of her time for design work. Jenn can advocate for herself if she needs to. The Blooms are different. They need someone to mediate with the world, or else they'll hurt themselves."

"So it's your job to carry them?"

"Somebody has to," she said. "The world needs their gifts. And I am not letting them blow this opportunity because of social awkwardness. Nor will I let anyone use them, or cheat them, or steal from them. I will flatten any son of a bitch who tries."

The smile that flashed over his face put her on the defensive. "What's so funny?"

He stopped by her door. "Nothing at all," he said. "I just hope the Blooms know how lucky they are to have you on their side."

Her face felt suddenly hot. "Okay. Well, thanks."

Her phone chirped in her bag, and she pulled it out and took a look at it, in case it was Ernest with a fresh crisis. It was a text from Drew.

Hey sis. Flying home day after tomorrow. Uncle Malcolm, Vann and Sophie coming home too. Bev wants us all back for the foundation gala. Jenna sends love. I'll call when we touch down. Be good. ttyl

She looked up at him. "Drew and Malcolm and the rest are coming home soon."

His face did not change expression. "Good. I'll be glad to have as many more people as possible circling the wagons around you until we solve this troll thing. Twenty minutes, okay? That gives us time to knot Bobby and Wilbur's ties and be downstairs on time. Knock on the inside door when you're ready."

"Sounds good," she said.

Once alone in her room, Ava wanted to have a mini meltdown, but she didn't have that luxury with mere minutes to put on her game face. The dress was an old favorite, midnight-blue silk with low-cut black velvet bodice. It fit looser than it should, since appetite-killing stress had been shrinking her lately. She twisted her hair up into a loose updo with dangling locks around her chin and put on some bolder makeup. Stepped into black heels, draped a blue silk and black velvet stole around her shoulders, and examined the results with a critical eye.

Whatever. The deep red of her lipstick made her skin ghostly pale, and her eyes looked worried and shadowy, but this was as good as it was going to get tonight.

She dropped her key card into her evening bag and rapped on the connecting door.

Zack opened it. He looked big and imposing and impossibly handsome in his slim-cut dark suit. He stared down at her, looking startled.

"What is it?" she demanded after an uncomfortably long pause. "Is something wrong? Is my makeup smeared? Have I a grown another head?"

"Nothing," he said gruffly. "Sorry. We better move if we want to get downstairs in time to help Bobby and Wilbur."

Ava squared her shoulders and ran her inner pep talk in her mind. She was woman to be reckoned with. The Bloom brothers' champion was on the rampage tonight.

Watch out, world.

It took longer than Zack anticipated to talk Bobby and Wilbur down off the ledge of their incipient panic attacks, but Ava pulled it off. Ernest had managed to smooth down the brothers' frizzy tufts into tidy ponytails, with the help of his own hair wax. The final emergency was Wilbur's nervous sweat attack, necessitating a last-minute fresh shirt.

Zack was fascinated with Ava's expert Bloom wrangling. She somehow managed to settle the nerves of the rattled brothers and bolster their confidence at the same time. Her nonstop patter as he knotted the Blooms' ties was both soothing and bracing.

The crowded ballroom downstairs was lit by an enormous art-piece chandelier with dangling prisms and lantern cutouts that spun, swirling slow, shifting patterns of gold-tinted light around the room like a lazy kaleidoscope. It was a perfect foil for Ava, who was already tinted gold. He did not understand how that dress stayed put on her stunning body. Women's mysteries. The big challenge was in not gawking like a meathead.

Dinner was pretty good, by mass banquet standards. Then the lights dimmed and it was time for the entertainment, a set from a hot new band, which consisted of a drummer, a guitarist and a waiflike young girl with blue hair in a baggy yellow athletic suit. She sang doleful but catchy ballads in a wispy little voice, about being lonesome, depressed, misunderstood, angry and ignored. Not exactly the message he wanted to dwell on right now, but it was something to stare at that wasn't Ava's décolletage.

Not that Ava would notice if he did gawk at her bosom. She was icily ignoring him. Embarrassed about their night together. Then, like a bad joke, the blue-haired girl belted out a song about her lover being embarrassed about having had sex with her. It was her big set closer. Sweet. His cup of awkward had officially overflowed.

The speechifying began, and all the big shots who had been involved with Future Innovation had to be heard from: a senator, a famous movie star, a university president, a handful of industry titans. They droned on and on.

Finally, the emcee announced the award and called up a famous biologist who had a highly popular science show on a big TV streaming platform to present it. Portia La Grasta walked up onto the stage in a sequined caftan, her long gray dreadlocks swaying, and proceeded to introduce the top six candidates. The audience watched a two-minute video presentation for each. It was all awesome stuff—a brilliant new solution for seawater desalination, a cutting-edge new plant micropropagation technique, a scalable hydrogen-powered vehicle, a hyperefficient desert solar farm. The Blooms were in good company.

Portia La Grasta finally brandished the oversize envelope. “And the Future Innovation prize for the most promising scientific innovation with the potential to transform our world goes to… Bobby and Wilbur Bloom, for the Desert Bloom project!”

Ava shot to her feet with a shriek of joy. The Bloom brothers jumped up, howling and capering and embracing each other. Pandemonium ensued. Wineglasses fell; wine was splashed. No one cared. A beaming Bobby and Wilbur made their way through the room and up onto the stage. Portia La Grasta and the emcee embraced them and handed Wilbur a plaque while Bobby stepped up to the mic, adjusting his glasses with shaking fingers.

“We, um, want to thank our lab techs, and the Maddox Hill Foundation for the research grants that made this work possible.” Bobby’s voice wobbled with emotion. “And a special thanks to our friend and publicist, Ava Maddox of Blazon PR and Branding, for telling our story and making everyone listen, and I mean from all the way back to the start of our research. None of this would have happened without her.”

“She’s brilliant,” Wilbur interjected, leaning into the mic. “And fabulous.” He pumped the plaque in the air. “This one’s for you, Ava! Thanks! You rock!”

The crowd roared with appreciative laughter, and the spotlight swung around the room and lit upon their table, illuminating Ava in all her glory. She seemed right at home in that brilliant beam of light, smiling and clapping, her eyes wet. She gracefully blew the Bloom brothers a kiss, like a blessing from a benevolent deity. The crowd roared and applauded, eating it up.

Not surprisingly, everybody wanted a piece of her and the Blooms after that. It took forever to grind through that process. After the official proceedings concluded, Zack waited while Ava and the Blooms accepted congratulations and collected business cards and fawning compliments. Trevor Wexford was there, Callista on his arm. She was looking fine in a flesh-toned, sequined, mostly see-through sheath that was far more low-cut than Ava's. The end visual result was naked but sparkling. Not a bad look for her, but he couldn't drag his eyes away from Ava to appreciate it. Which Callista of course noticed.

At long last, he had the whole lot of them all herded into the elevator. The Blooms were still bubbling with euphoria, talking a mile a minute.

"All the big investors want us now," Wilbur exulted. "We have a meeting with Wexford next week! And four others!"

"Be careful with those guys," Ava reminded them. "They are predatory animals. They will chew you up and spit out your bones if you let them."

"But they won't, because thanks to you, we have great lawyers lined up to help us negotiate," Bobby assured her.

The elevator door opened, and Zack stuck his foot in the door to give them time for the last round of emotional hugs. Then the door shut behind Ernest and the Blooms, leaving Ava and Zack alone. The elevator ascended, in cut-it-with-a-knife silence.

He worked up the nerve to speak as they walked toward the rooms. "I'm glad the Blooms had the presence of mind to thank you properly. When Bobby took the mic, I was braced for anything. But he nailed it. Short, sweet and appropriate. You deserved it."

She shrugged. "Thanks, but I just polish the gems. I don't make them."

"You know damn well it's more than that. Particularly with the Blooms."

Ava swiped her key card, opened the door and beckoned him in. He willed his heart to stop racing as he followed her in. His heart ignored the directive.

Ava laid down her evening bag. "It's a rush to get a compliment from you, considering."

"Considering what?"

Her eyebrow tilted up. "Don't play dumb. You've been radiating Arctic disapproval at me for two days. It makes it hard to concentrate."

"I'm sorry you feel that way," he said stiffly. "I didn't mean to make you uncomfortable. And you're wrong. I don't disapprove of you. On the contrary."

"How can you say that after what happened with Craig? And two days of glaring and grunted monosyllables? Get real."

Zack's hands clenched as the energy built up. "Ava," he said tightly. "That's not fair. You ask too damn much. I've got to protect myself somehow."

She threw up her hands, baffled. "Protect yourself from what?"

"From you," he blurted out. "I've been trying for years. I should have kept trying, but no. I gave in. And sure enough, I regret how it played out."

Her stole dropped with a whispery thud around her feet.

"I should never have gone to bed with you," he said. "I know myself. I can't play it cool, pretend it's no big deal. I suck at that. I get that this was a one and done for you. But what a surprise, I'm not okay with it. I'm an all-or-nothing kind of guy."

"Am I really such a heartless femme fatale?" she asked.

"For me, you sure as hell are," he said. "I've had a massive crush on you ever since we first met. You must have noticed. It had to be impossible to miss."

"Um…actually," she faltered. "I, um, I didn't know that. In the least."

His voice was bitter. "Like always, I've got champagne tastes and a lemonade budget. I'm your brother's battle buddy from Iraq, and you're, like, Marie freaking Antoinette. It was stupid to lay myself wide-open, but I can't take it back. We're both embarrassed. But we'll live. After tomorrow, we'll avoid each other and move on."

"Zack…but I—"

"I didn't make mean to make this harder for you," he said. "I'll go now."

He turned toward the connecting door, but she lunged toward him, grabbing his wrist. "Wait," she said. "You've got it wrong. I don't want to move on."

His heart did that triple somersault again, then started off on a frantic gallop.

Her slender hand clamped around his wrist, although her fingers couldn't close around it. Her eyes were wet. *Oh, man.* He was out of his depth and sinking fast.

"Ava," he said. "Really. Don't sweat it. I won't give you a hard time. I get it."

"No. You don't get it, Zack. You don't get a goddamn thing."

"What, then? Help me out here. What is it I don't get?"

"How much I want this." Her voice quivered and broke. "But I just can't have it."

"Can't have what? Me?" He was utterly confused. "Why not? Here I am, on my knees. If you want me, what the hell is holding you back?"

She made a choked, desperate sound. "Me. It's just… me."

He was silent for a moment. "Please, don't give me the old it's-not-you-it's-me treatment," he said. "That never comforted anybody."

"I wasn't trying to comfort you. Far from it. Would you be quiet and let me explain?"

Zack made a lip-zipping gesture and gestured for her to go ahead.

Ava twisted her hands together until her fingers turned white. "That thing that happened the other morning," she said. "That's me every morning. I'm always like that."

"You mean…"

"Miserable. Nights and early mornings are just bad for me. I sink really low. But it has nothing to do with you. It's been years since I let anyone stay a whole night with me. I'm always in that dark place in the morning. If I sleep at all, I have screaming nightmares. Usually my parents' plane going down." She stopped to calm her shaking voice.

"Did you have that nightmare the other morning, when you woke up with me?"

"Yes," she said. "It was a bad one. Sometimes I can keep myself from screaming, but I can't stop the tears. Either one is a huge buzzkill for anyone sharing my bed. And even if I skip the nightmare, I still have the feeling. It spills all over anyone who's with me. I just can't seem to hide it, or control it."

He waited for more. "Tell me about the feeling," he urged.

She hesitated. "It's like the tide going out," she said. "In a bad way. Something vital is draining away, no way to stop it, and I'm stranded on the rocks. I'm just not fit to be seen like that. And I don't want to burden anyone with it. Certainly not you."

"Oh, baby," he whispered.

"I'm not looking for pity," she said forcefully. "I'm very grateful for what life has given me. I'm healthy, privileged. Pampered, even. I have people who care about me, and I have work that I like, and I'm grateful for all that. No one has to tell me."

"I wasn't going to tell you that," he said. "Have you talked to anyone?"

"Yes. I've tried various things. Therapy, medications. So far, nothing works all that well. Exercise helps some. And being really busy. During the day, I can hold it off if I just keep moving. Sometimes it feels like my life is one long con job. Me, running around to show the world that I am just fine, thank you very much. Busy, busy. Sparkle, sparkle."

"That sounds exhausting," he said.

"Oh, it is," she said fervently. "But when I wake up

in the night, I just can't fake it. Not even with you. I haven't had a boyfriend in years. I can only go so far with someone, and then it all just…falls apart on me."

"I'm so sorry," he said gently.

"But you want to know something funny? I've never wanted to try again as much as I want to try with you. But I can't run my con on you, Zack. Not at all. Not even during the daytime. It just doesn't work. I feel completely naked. I can't hide it from you."

"So don't," he said simply.

"Oh, stop," she muttered. "You don't know what you're asking."

"So teach me. I'm listening. My ears are wide-open."

"I told you," she said. "Believe me. It's not pretty."

"You're not pretty, Av, you're beautiful. Even when you're sad. Even when you're falling apart. You're amazing, and brave, and tough. You leave me speechless."

Ava shook with silent laughter. "I wouldn't call you speechless, Zack. You sound pretty damn eloquent to me."

Her hand was still clutching his arm. She seemed to have forgotten it was there. Zack rotated his arm, careful not to break her grip, and clasped her wrist gently with his fingers.

"You know what?" He bent down, pressing a kiss against the back of her hand. "If I had a pool behind me right now, I'd pull you into it and kiss you senseless."

Ava's mouth opened, forming words with no sound. Her eyes were wide, dilated.

"Well, actually," she whispered. "We don't need a pool for that."

Twelve

And in a heartbeat, they were at it. With all the thundering intensity of racehorses out of the gate.

Ava just wrapped her arms around his neck and hung on. She felt cherished by the way he cradled her head, made love to her mouth. She felt precious, adored, desired. His craving intensified her own. Reality could rip and tear under this kind of pressure.

But it didn't. It stayed intact. Nothing would fall to pieces with Zack around to hold it together. He had absolute command of himself.

His long, stiff erection burned through the fabric of her dress, and she burned to get closer to him. She wound one of her legs around him, and when that wasn't enough, she clutched his shoulders and hiked up the other one, too.

Zack let out a hoarse growl of approval and hoisted her up so that her legs were wrapped around his waist, not his thighs, and she was rubbing the stiff bulge of his erection right against the party spot. Straddling him, squeezing. He cupped her bottom and helped, grinding their bodies together. Driving her to distraction.

So good. She moved helplessly, driven by some primal imperative, one she couldn't control. She clutched him, panting as her climax build up, and up…and shattered, in a blaze of stars. Huge pleasure pulsed through her.

It washed the whole world clean.

After, her shaking legs were still twined around him, but she was limp and soft. Zack hoisted her up and carried her to the bed, laying her down with exquisite gentleness. He positioned himself above her, distributing his weight right where she needed to feel it, and moved, expertly, deepening the pressure. A slow, sensual pulse and grind, rocking and surging. Working her right back up to a screaming pitch of excitement.

Soon, she was clutching his shirt, nails digging in, scrabbling for the buttons. "Get this shirt off. I want to run my hands over your chest. I need to feel your skin."

"As my lady commands." He lifted himself up, flung off the suit jacket. Made short work of the buttons.

Ava took the opportunity to pry open the buckles of her ankle straps, staring at him as she tossed her shoes away. Zack wrenched his belt loose and sat down next to her. He slid his fingers into her hair with a groan, pulling the pins out and unwinding the locks, sliding them through his fingers. He slowly stroked her skin into shuddering bliss as he pushed the black velvet straps over her arms, tugging the bodice of her dress down until it cradled her bare breasts.

He pressed his face against her breasts with a groan, kissing her. Caressing her sensitive skin with his swirling, skillful tongue.

She clutched his shoulders. Her breath heaved in her chest at the incredible sensations. Light, heat, pleasure. The stiffened tips of her breasts seemed to glow with delight at his passionate appreciation. Then he slid his hand up the inside of her thigh, stroking her mound, then sliding under the elastic of the damp fabric. Tugging her panties off. Then opening her. Entering her with skillful fingers. Thrusting, caressing, finding the perfect spot. *Oh, please.* A shocked moan, a ripple of sweet surrender and her legs opened, lifting eagerly for more of the same. "Help me get this dress off," she said breathlessly.

"No," Zack said. "The dress totally does it for me. With your breasts bare like that, the skirt thrown up." He pushed her thighs open. "So perfect. Silky smooth." He thrust his finger inside her, tenderly, rhythmically, seeking out the sweet spots that made her shiver and squirm and gasp. "Hot and tight. You hug me. I'm about to come right now."

"Don't you dare waste it. Get your pants off and stop driving me crazy, you big tease. I want all that excellent bounty for me, me, me. At my service. You get me?"

"But I love driving you crazy. How about we go for at least one more of those supernova orgasms before we move on to the next part of the evening's entertainment?"

She reached up to cup his face. "I want to supernova with you," she told him. "We've got the rest of the night for the fun and games."

His eyes lit up. "Well, then. If you put it that way."

Zack slid off the bed, kicked off his shoes and swiftly shucked pants, socks and briefs, freeing that impressive erection. There was no doubt at all about his enthusiasm.

"Get over here, you," she said. "Give me what's mine."

He complied in an instant, bearing her over backward onto the bed.

"First, the mutual supernova," he murmured. "Then the fun and games."

He positioned himself on his knees between her legs, lifting her up so he could use the tip of his broad shaft to caress her secret inner flesh. Swirling, teasing, stroking. She lifted herself, silently straining for more as he nudged inside and pressed deeper.

They both cried out as he entered her, the pleasure was so intense. Their hands clenched, shaking with emotion as they found the rhythm together. Deep… slick…heavy strokes. The only sounds the faint squeak of the bed and their panting breath. They were beyond words, merged, in the danger zone where she was stark naked, revealed to him. All her hopes and fears and pain, all her desires and fantasies, wide-open to him.

And safe, with him.

Every deep thrust of his big body brought the truth closer. Each tender, slick stroke of pure pleasure, as deep and intimate as a kiss. Revelation after sweet, passionate, tender revelation. Zack sensed the explosion building and let go of his own control, racing for the finish. Their beautiful supernova, getting closer.

Her shining light in the darkness.

Thirteen

Zack cradled Ava's soft, warm weight, staring at the ceiling in stunned disbelief.

It was real. It had actually happened. Over and over. Ava had drifted off after their last bout of luxurious lovemaking, her slender, silken limbs twined trustingly around his.

It was too good to be true. He was afraid to let himself believe it. He'd tried to be lighthearted and playful. Fun and games, that was the vibe he'd shot for, but he hadn't hit the mark. Not even close. Every time they came together, they were seized by that crazy, desperate, end-of-the-world intensity. Every time it got wilder, more abandoned.

There was no taking the edge off these feelings. No breaking this tension. No end to how deep he could go. It was bottomless. It left him in a state of terrified joy.

He needed to knock down walls inside his head make enough room for her there. He never wanted her to feel cramped. Ava was special. She had a destiny to fulfill, and he wanted her to reach it.

He wanted to see her shine like the goddamn star that she was.

He was too stirred up to even think of sleeping. The sky had started to lighten when he felt her stir in his arms and then stretch.

He felt the exact moment when she realized where she was, and he felt her stiffen.

This was the moment of truth. He steeled himself for freaking anything at all.

Ava pushed back from his tight embrace, propping herself up onto her elbow, and gave him a shy, tentative smile. "Hi," she said softly. "How long was I out?"

"Maybe three hours," he told her. "Maybe more. Sleep some more. It's still early."

Ava laughed. "You know, of course, that it's a miracle I slept that long at all," she told him. She sat up, swinging her legs around, her back to him, her long, honey-blond curls catching the light that still filtered out the bathroom door.

Zack waited for a moment before he worked up the nerve to break the silence. "So?" he asked her. "How do you feel right now? Did the tide go out?"

She looked back over her shoulder with wide, wondering eyes. "No," she said softly. "I feel…okay. Better than okay. I can hardly believe it. I actually feel pretty good."

"It wouldn't scare me, if you were struggling," he told her. "It's sure to show up again from time to time.

Don't try to hide it from me. We'll cope with it together."

She gave him a smile so sweet, it made his heart squeeze and twist. "Thanks. I will. But I'm telling you the absolute truth, I swear. I feel good today. It's amazing."

He grinned, ridiculously happy. "Awesome."

"Yeah, fingers crossed. I don't know how long it'll last, or what it means, but I'll take it."

"I know exactly what it means," he told her.

Ava gave him a teasing smile, head tilted. "Oh, really, Zack? Enlighten me."

Now she was messing with him for making pronouncements, but he was too euphoric to mind. "Three things," he said. "It means that it can get better. It doesn't define you. And it won't limit you. That's what it means. Good, hopeful, positive things."

Her smile widened into a grin, showing her gorgeous white teeth. "Why, you seductive bastard," she said. "Whispering your irresistible sweet nothings in my ear."

"What can I say," he murmured. "We all have our gifts."

"True thing." Ava pulled the cover down, baring his body, and swung her shapely thigh over his, straddling him. She leaned over him, stroking his chest. Reaching down to grasp his thick, pulsing shaft. Boldly stroking it. "So, ah…speaking of gifts…"

"Again?" he asked hopefully. "You're not tired?"

"Not yet." Her voice was husky and seductive. "I like feeling this way." She wiggled down his thighs, leaning over to let her satiny hair brush down his chest. "I have a few sweet nothings of my own for you, Zack."

Then she put her hot mouth to him, and all he could do was clutch the sheets, shudder and gasp.

Something felt strange when Ava opened her eyes. It took her a while to figure out what it was. It wasn't so much the marvelous novelty of being in the arms of a gorgeous man, though that itself was quite excellent.

It was the slice of light that slanted down from between the heavy blackout curtains. It was brilliantly bright. Not the usual faint, grayish glow of dawn.

She twisted around, squinting through her tousled mop of hair at the digital clock, and gasped. "Ten fifteen a.m.?" she squawked. "Oh my God! Holy…freaking…*crap*!"

Zack jumped as she leaped up. "What the hell? Are you okay? What's wrong?"

"I'm three hours late, that's what's wrong!"

"Oh. Okay." Zack rubbed his eyes and sat up. "You didn't set an alarm clock?"

"No! Why would I? I barely ever sleep! I've never needed an alarm in my whole life! I don't even know how the alarm clock function on my smartphone works!"

"Oh. So rolling around in bed all night with me makes you oversleep? Cool."

Ava grabbed a pillow and swung it at his head. "Don't you dare get smug about that."

"Don't worry," he urged. "The Blooms will survive for a few hours on their own. They're the darlings of Future Innovation. They're probably down there holding court with hungry venture capitalists right now."

"Uh-huh, right! With no contract lawyers present. That's exactly the problem."

"I see. Well, Ernest is with them, right? He'll run interference."

"Yeah, and he's probably wondering where the hell I am. Get dressed quick, you lazy, lounging naked man. As soon as I'm decent, I am out the door, with or without you."

"You're not going anywhere alone," he told her sternly.

She stopped at the bathroom door. "Actually, Zack. Drew and Uncle Malcolm will soon be getting on a plane headed back to the States, remember. And this new development will eliminate all your bully leverage."

"Oh, yeah? Meaning?"

She smiled. "Meaning, your carrot-and-stick routine will soon be officially obsolete, big guy," she informed him softly. "And I, for one, will not miss it."

"Ava," he said, in a warning tone. "Nothing has changed. You need to stay safe."

"I guess you'll just have to come up with a clever, creative new way to manage me after that," she said throatily. "With a new carrot, or, ah…a new stick." Her eyes dropped to his lap. "A nice, big, substantial one."

His erection tented the sheet up, and he sat up, all smoldering, sexy bedroom eyes.

"Let Ernest handle things down there," he said. "Get over here and let's see how this new leverage is going to work. We should start working out the kinks."

Ava backed away, laughing, her face already hot.

"Kinks, ha! Put it on ice, you crazy sex demon. I have a counterproposal for you."

He gave her a lazy grin that made her heart throb heavily. "I'm listening."

"When we get back to Seattle, come to my house," she said. "We'll open a bottle of wine. Light some candles. Order some good takeout. Maybe run a bath. I have a big old claw-foot cast iron bathtub, big enough for two, if they're very friendly. And we can discuss our complicated new power arrangement for hours. Or even, um…days."

"What time is our plane?" he asked roughly. "I can't wait to get started."

When the bathroom door closed, she was giggling like a schoolgirl.

Fourteen

"So which of your hot evening dresses are you wearing to the foundation gala?"

Ava smiled across the restaurant table at Zack. "I'm still vacillating between the black beaded velvet or the crimson taffeta with the big full skirt."

"You look awesome in both," Zack said. "But the strapless red one just does something to me. I don't understand how those things stay up."

"Pro trick," Ava said. "Don't let your boyfriend touch you until you get home."

"Whoa," he said. "That'll be a challenge."

"You'll get your moment later, I promise. That deep crimson is my absolute favorite. It's my signature color."

Ava twined her fingers with Zack's and leaned toward him over the espresso cups and the plate of lemon profiterole they'd shared. It was the same restaurant he'd chosen for their first evening together, hardly more than a week ago. This place had become their go-to spot for workday lunches.

"I have to get back to work," Ava said regretfully. "I told Ernest to check on Wilbur and Bobby, and sure enough, they have a wardrobe crisis. He's been sending me frantic texts about last-minute tuxedos for them. The rest of my afternoon will be spent on damage control. No rest for the wicked."

"Gregson will accompany you anytime you leave the Blazon office, right?"

Ava slid her foot out of her shoe and ran it up the side of his calf. "Of course," she said. "I know you want me to keep me safe, but I think my trolls are losing interest. There's been no new activity for the last few days. Maybe the worst is over."

He pulled her hand up and kissed it. "I still don't want you to risk it."

"I won't," she assured him. "I'll be careful, I promise."

"Meet you after work?" he offered. "Want to get dinner?"

"Or we could just meet at my place. I might not get back to Gilchrist House at all if I have to find tuxes for the Blooms. And I'll be famished for you."

Zack's smile widened. "Your place. Keep me posted on your timing. We'll figure out dinner later."

"Perfect." She beamed as she sipped her espresso.

Strange, to be so giddy and giggly after all her troubles, but she was having more fun than she'd ever had in her life. Apart from being a total god in bed, Zack was fun to be with. Smart, funny, thoughtful, opinionated. They had spirited disputes about movies, music, current events and everything else under the sun. She loved cooking with him, lolling in bed with him, sipping coffee. He saw who she really was, and he seemed to like it, just as she liked him. And between frequent erotic interludes, she slept like a rock and woke deliciously rested, smiling and ready for anything.

It felt incredible. She was flying high. Hoping desperately not to crash.

Vikram's crew of close protection agents covered her during Zack's work hours. At every other moment, Zack covered her himself. Quite literally, much of the time. To her knee-wobbling, thigh-clenching, toe-curling delight.

Her phone did its classic guitar riff ringtone in her purse, and she dug around for it.

"Dammit, Ernest, stop hounding me," she muttered. "I'll get there when I get there." She pulled out the phone and froze. "Not Ernest," she said blankly. "It's Drew."

In the startled silence that followed, the guitar riff played again. Again.

"You going to answer that?" Zack asked.

"Of course," Ava said.

It rang again. "Are you going to tell him about us?" Zack asked.

"When the time is right." Ava hit Talk. "Hey, big brother! I meant to call, but I thought you'd be conked out. Have you and Jenna emerged from the fog of jet lag?"

"Hell, no," Drew replied. "It feels like I'm walking on the moon. But I'm sharp enough to be pissed off at you."

Ava rolled her eyes and sighed silently. "So what else is new."

"How is it that I just learned about your trolls now?"

Drew demanded. "Sophie told me this morning! The security team that Zack appointed for you filled her in. You should have told us!"

"I didn't want to wreck your honeymoon, Drew."

"That's my decision to make, and Jenna feels the same way. We can go play on a beach anytime, Av. Nothing is more important to us than you being safe. Nothing. Get it?"

Aww. It sucked to be yelled at, but she was used to it, and she was touched that Drew felt so passionately about keeping her safe. "I appreciate the sentiment," she told him. "And I'm glad you're back. I really missed you guys. But I'm fine. Zack had my back."

He grunted under his breath. "We'll discuss it with Uncle Malcolm tonight. Dinner at his house on the island. I'll pick you up. Bring everything you'll need to dress for the gala tomorrow night. We'll all go together from Vashon."

"But, ah…actually, tonight I've got a thing that I need to…"

"Cancel it. Malcolm is on edge already. He wants to formally welcome Sophie into the family tonight, and you have absolutely got to be there. No choice."

Ava sighed. "Whatever. It'll be great to see you, even spitting mad. Love you, bro."

She ended the call and dropped the phone into her purse. "I'm so sorry," she said to Zack ruefully. "I'm in for it tonight. Drew is taking me to Uncle Malcolm's house on Vashon for a welcome-Sophie-to-the-family dinner. Or maybe it'll be more like a rake-Ava-over-the-coals dinner."

"Are you ready to let them know that we're seeing each other?"

Ava considered her words. This was his tender spot, the one she had to tiptoe around. "Let's not steal Sophie and Vann's thunder yet. They're just starting to plan their wedding."

"So you're still nervous."

"No," she retorted. "Not nervous, exactly. It's just that this is private. It's fresh and new. It's also kind of miraculous, and outside eyes wouldn't be able to see that."

"It might be fresh and new," Zack said. "But it's not delicate."

Ava squeezed his hand. "By no means," she said. "I just want to leave it unmolested for a while longer before I expose it to Uncle Malcolm's judgment."

"So you think he won't approve?" Zack said.

"Of me, no," she said ruefully. "Never. Just out of habit. It's beyond him to approve of anything I decide to do. He's far more likely to approve of you, Zack. He likes you. He thinks you're rock solid. Otherwise you wouldn't be the company's CSO."

"Maybe I should come with you tonight," he said.

"Stay clear," Ava advised him. "It's going to be stressful. He'll be horrified at my trolls, and he will almost certainly blame me for it. You know, my unfortunate life choices that opened me up to that kind of abuse. So spare yourself."

"I should be standing with you for that," he said.

"And you will, tomorrow. At the gala, and going forward," she assured him.

They dealt with the bill and strolled back toward Gilchrist House holding hands. Gregson, her bodyguard for the day, waited for her at the front entrance as requested.

She smiled at him. "'Bye," she whispered. "Until tomorrow."

Zack pulled her close and gave her a fierce kiss that promised infinite sensual bliss. The man was voracious. He couldn't get enough, and neither could she. She stepped back gasping for breath.

Tomorrow couldn't come too soon.

Imagining that strapless crimson evening gown clinging to Ava's stunning body soon became impractical for a city street in broad daylight. He had to do deep breathing to chill himself down to normal dimensions. In the middle of that effort at self-mastery, his eyes fell on the display window of a high-end jewelry store.

He gazed thoughtfully at the gems in the window, thinking about Ava's red dress. *It's my signature color.* He went inside and approached the woman behind the counter.

"Show me your ruby rings," he said.

Some time later, he'd narrowed the choices down to a few front-runners. He had a clear favorite, by far the most expensive of the lot. But he made better money at this job then he'd ever dreamed of making, and he didn't have time to spend much of it. He could afford something worthy of her beauty. Better yet, something that would look good with that red dress, and with those gold and ruby drop earrings Ava often wore. She looked so good in those and absolutely nothing else. It was a great look for her.

A ruby ring would be a perfect addition to that winning ensemble.

The setting was modern, a twisted rope of differently colored golds, with a big ruby nested inside it. It was bold, eye-catching, unique, unusual. Risky. Like Ava.

If it was the wrong ring, he'd bring her back and let her pick out whatever she wanted. Probably he was pushing his luck. It might be too soon. But he knew where he wanted this to go. He'd always known, if he was honest with himself.

His phone buzzed, and he pulled it out, hoping for Ava. No such luck. Drew.

Zack hit Talk. "Hey, man," he said. "Welcome back."

"Where the hell have you been?" Drew sounded peeved. "I drag my tired, jet-lagged ass into the office today to talk to you and find that you've disappeared for a long lunch? Since when do you take long lunches?"

"I had some business to deal with," Zack said. "We didn't expect you guys back for another week or so. Did the honeymoon go well?"

"The honeymoon was awesome. We were summoned back by royal decree. Bev Hill insisted that Jenna and I be present for the foundation gala, and Ava's been telling me that I should talk to the Bloom brothers about Beyond Earth before they get too rich and famous to talk to me. From the looks of things, it might already be too late. In any case, we'll be there tomorrow night, jet lag and all."

"Great," Zack said. "Looking forward to seeing you."

"So tell me about this security issue that Ava has?" Drew's voice had an edge. "How the hell did you decide not to let Malcolm and me know about that situation?"

"Ava didn't want to disturb you guys. She was afraid you'd cut short your travels."

Drew let out a grunt of disapproval. "That decision

was not Ava's to make. Going forward, when it come to my family's security, keep me in the loop. Always."

"Understood," Zack said.

"We'll discuss it tonight at Uncle Malcolm's," Drew said. "He told me to invite you. It'll be Jenna and me, Ava, Uncle Malcolm, Sophie, and Vann. Pack what you need for the gala, because it'll be too late after dinner to get the ferry to the mainland. There's room at Malcolm's house. We'll have the housekeeper make up a room."

"So Malcolm wants to scold me about Ava's problem?"

"I think his exact words were 'Tell Zack to get his secretive ass out to the island tonight, or we will have a problem.'"

"Ah," Zack said. "Great. Fun times ahead."

"Definitely, but the food will be good, and Malcolm shipped a bunch of cases of really good Italian wine back from Positano. Just get buzzed and tune him out. That's what Ava and I do." Drew paused. "Of course, that'll be after I pound you myself for not keeping me clued in. You can relax and get drunk when honor has been satisfied."

Zack was too busy secretly exulting at the idea of being in the same house with Ava tonight to be troubled by that prospect. "Do what you have to do. I'm there for it."

He slid his phone into his pocket and pulled out his wallet as he turned back to the woman behind the jewelry counter. He pointed at the most expensive ruby ring.

"I'll take that one," he said.

Fifteen

"I told you, Uncle," Ava repeated stubbornly. "As soon as I got nervous, I went to Zack and asked his advice. I was reluctant to interrupt your important trip for something unimportant. I was absolutely covered, so I just don't know what you're so upset about."

"I don't like being kept in the dark!" Uncle Malcolm sputtered. "I saw the disgusting things they posted. I want to hunt that filth down and crush them!"

Ava opened her mouth to snap back but stopped herself. After a week with Zack with her emotional defenses down, she saw her uncle's face differently. For the first time, she saw the fear behind his bluster.

"I'm fine," she said gently. "And I've been careful. Since I told Zack my problem, I have not been left alone without protection even once."

"I hate it. I hate that you were exposed to something so obscene!"

"I'm tough," she assured him. "I'm a Maddox, Uncle. Welsh warrior stock. Name-calling doesn't rattle me. You were the one who taught me not to back down from a bully."

"Well." Malcolm harrumphed. "This is quite different."

"As far as I'm concerned, you did the right things." Sophie's mild, soothing tone indicated that even after only a few weeks of acquaintance with her biological father, her cousin had already firmly grasped the basics of Malcolm management.

Probably better than Ava had over the course of a lifetime.

Not for the first time, it occurred to her that it was a good thing Sophie was such fun to be with in her own right, or Ava would've been hopelessly jealous. Her own relationship with her uncle had always been fraught with tension, but Sophie had swiftly forged a real friendship with her biological father. They enjoyed each other's company, and Malcolm did not harangue or criticize Sophie the way he did Ava and Drew.

Maybe because he hadn't seen her through her awkward teens. Sophie had already been a highly functioning adult when he met her. Like Athena, springing from the head of Zeus fully formed. Brilliant, funny, gorgeous. Vann Acosta, Maddox Hill's chief financial officer, had fallen for her like a ton of broken rock. Vann had always struck Ava as cool and distant, so it warmed her heart to watch him so devoted to her. Crazy in love.

Even now, Vann was stuck to Sophie like glue, arm

wound through her arm, thigh pressed against hers, nuzzling her hair. Not that Ava could criticize. If she were alone with Zack right now, she would climb that guy like a tree.

"Nothing bad happened," Jenna pointed out to the room at large. "And nothing bad will happen now that her entire family is lurking around every corner. Malcolm, look at you. You got a tan in Positano. It looks good on you!"

"My dermatologist would disagree in the strongest of terms," Malcolm grumbled. "It was impossible to avoid. And believe me, I tried. The place is a damn oven."

They heard the front door open. Ava heard her brother talking. Then Drew walked in, followed by Zack. Seeing him unexpectedly made her heart bump hard in her chest.

"There you are!" Malcolm said. "Good! I have some things to say to you."

"You didn't say you were coming," Ava blurted. "You should have texted me."

An odd silence followed her words, but Malcolm quickly broke it. "So, Zack! What the hell do you have to say for yourself? Keeping secrets from us?"

Zack gazed calmly back at him. "I stand by all my choices."

"Really? You concluded that keeping us all in the dark about a security issue in our immediate family was a good choice? I should have you fired!"

Zack looked unrepentant. "That would be a shame. But do what you need to do."

Ava shot to her feet. "Like hell will you fire him! That would be stupid. He has been nothing but professional. He made me his first priority, the minute I told him about my problem, so back off!"

The antique mantel clock over the fireplace tick-ticked loudly after her words.

"Ava," Zack said. "You don't have to defend me. I'll be fine."

"I'm finished with this conversation," she announced. "Everyone just be polite and speak of other things, or Zack and I will catch the ferry back to the city right now."

"You will do no such thing," Malcolm snapped. "We are going to have dinner together tonight, like a civilized family. Jeffries?" he bawled out. "Where are you?"

The bald head of Malcolm's butler poked through the door. "Yes, Mr. Maddox?"

"Tell Mrs. Alvarez we're ready for dinner as soon as she can serve it."

"Yes, sir."

Dinner was surreal. Ava had the strangest sensation that she was floating over the table, watching all of them from a distance. Her uncle had a talented cook, and the wine was great, but she couldn't seem to get anything down.

The one bright spot was when Jenna stood up, holding Drew's hand, and announced that she was pregnant. She was going to be an aunt. Ava did all the requisite hugging and jumping and crying, but some part of her still watched it all from afar.

Jenna and Drew's announcement put Uncle Malcolm in a somewhat better humor, at least for him. Zack seemed perfectly at ease, talking shop with Sophie about cybersecurity, analyzing Ava's online harassment problem for them. Then he started telling funny stories about the Blooms' antics at the trade show. The tale of the Bloom brothers' fateful encounter with Callista Wexford made everyone laugh.

Everyone managed to relax at dinner except for her. Lucky them.

She still felt like she was braced for a blow, but she had no clue from what quarter.

Zack waited on the freshly made bed in the guest room, staring at the little velvet box in his hand.

Maybe he should wait to take this step. But he'd been waiting for a goddamn decade. Trying so hard not to feel it. And now that he finally had permission, all the feelings were rushing out at once, full force, like a flash flood.

He knew exactly what he wanted. He was dead sure that asking Ava to marry him was his only chance at happiness. Even so, asking the question was going to take all his balls and then some.

He unzipped the side pocket on his athletic pants and stowed the ring box there. It would be ready whenever he worked up the nerve.

He waited until the silence had fully settled in, then made his quiet way, barefoot, down to the end of the upstairs corridor. Ava's was the only bedroom that had a thin slice of light shining out of it. The other two couples were tucked behind closed doors, but Ava had left him a beacon.

He looked inside the narrow opening and pushed the door open.

She stood by the window, looking out at the trees

below her window. She wore turquoise-blue silk pajamas. They struck him as incredibly sexy, but as Ava had pointed out, every damn thing she wore had that effect on him. Even her ripped-up jeans with the paint stains made him get hot. If Ava wore it, it was sexy.

The room was large and pretty, furnished with a big four-poster canopy bed with a heap of lace-trimmed pillows on it and an antique patchwork quilt. There was a marble-topped dresser drawer, and a vanity with a tall, narrow makeup mirror with those lights all the way around it, like the backstage dressing room of a theater. The vanity lights were the only lamp lit, and they gave the room a soft golden glow.

Or maybe that was Ava herself. "Hey," he said.

Ava turned and smiled. "What took you so long? Come in and shut the door."

He walked over to the window and slid his hand under the warm mass of her beautiful hair. She was vibrating with tension.

"You shouldn't let Malcolm upset you," he said. "He just had to unload."

Her shoulders twitched in an angry shrug. "It pissed me off that he attacked you. He's so childish, with his goddamn tantrums. Threatening to fire you, my ass."

"It's just what he does," Zack said. "He fired Drew after that thing with Harold and his showgirl, remember? And he fired Vann, too, after that business with Tim and the deep fakes. I'm just part of that exclusive club now. Yay, me."

She harrumphed. "I appreciate your positive attitude and capacity for forgiveness, but it still just bugs me. And I bug him. I always have, and now look at him. He finally gets the perfect daughter, dropped from the heavens into his lap, boom. Instead of a couple of screwups that he inherited from his brother, like me and Drew."

"Oh, come on. You're not screwups. You love Sophie."

"Sure. What's not to love? She's brilliant, awesome, talented, wonderful."

"Yeah, and so are you," Zack said. "You're incredible. You dazzle me."

She laughed under her breath. "Aw, thanks. So I'm a little jealous and territorial after all. I'm not proud of it, but it bugs me that he brings this shiny, perfect new daughter home and tears me to pieces in front of her. Like any of this crap is my fault."

"He's scared and angry, like I was," Zack said. "Let him have his freak-out. It'll pass. Sophie certainly isn't judging you. She's a security expert. She's on your side."

Ava paced up and down the room as he watched. She stopped in front of the vanity, staring into it with eyes that looked faraway and sad. Which was unacceptable.

Zack came up behind her, dropping a soft kiss against the back of her head.

"It's more than that, isn't it?" he asked.

"No. I mean, yes," she admitted. "This is where Drew and I came to live after my parents died. I spent some very bad nights in this room. My ghosts haunt me harder here."

Zack slid his arms around her waist and tugged her until she leaned against him and her head rested on his shoulder. "I remember the very first time I saw this house," he told her. "It also happened to be the first time I ever saw you."

She looked up. "Oh, yeah. I remember. It was summertime, right? And Drew brought you and Vann home for a barbecue. Wasn't that right after you'd been hired to be a bodyguard for Hendrick when he went to South Africa?"

"Yeah, exactly. Drew was still in architecture school. Vann and I stayed overnight. My mind was blown by this place. I mean, I knew Drew came from money, that his uncle was a big-shot architect. We'd talked about his family. But seeing this house, the grounds, the indoor pool, the staff… It was still a big shock to my system. Vann had been working in the accounting department at Maddox Hill for a year, so he was used to it. I tried to act like it was no big deal. Then someone dropped you off at the driveway. You saw us as you went to the house and changed course. Came sashaying toward us across the lawn."

"Oh." She grinned at him. "Wow. Did I sashay?"

"You totally did," he assured her. "A sexy, hip-swaying femme fatale sashay, in that tight little sundress. Remember it? Big red flowers on black. Short skirt. Your hair, swaying in the breeze. A golden goddess bestowing her grace upon us unworthy mortals."

Ava shook with silent laughter. "Don't overdo it."

"I swear to God," he said. "I practically fell to my knees then and there. Drew introduced you. He was classy about it, but stern. This was his little sister, big emphasis on the 'little.' Just turned eighteen. Just graduated from high school. On her way to university. The message was clear. Hands off, eyes down, and don't even think about it."

"He's always been overprotective, but he's got nothing on you," she teased.

"I think they put me in that same guest bedroom I have now," he said, his hands settling into the deep, sexy curve of her waist. "But I couldn't sleep. I tossed and turned. Dreaming of all the hot scenarios, if I were that kind of guy."

"Yeah?" Her eyes had that sultry glow that made him crazy. "What kind of hot scenarios? What kind of guy? Be specific."

"Oh, real classic stuff." He turned his head and found the warm, sweet skin of her throat with his lips. "I thought about tossing pebbles at your window, luring you outside. Maybe to that pool. Or else sneaking into your room." He unfastened the buttons of the silky pajama top and slid it off her smooth, warm shoulders, cupping her perfect breasts. "The idea was to worship your entire body with my mouth."

Ava swayed on her feet, her breath ragged. He clamped her closer to the front of his body and slid his hand down into the loose waistband of her pajama pants, caressing her skin, the thin stretchy lace and, under that, the warm little swatch of springy ringlets decorating her sweet, secret folds.

He got his fingers under the lace and probed deeper, caressing her slick, tight-furled folds with his fingers until she trembled. Taking his time, teasing and demanding.

When the first orgasm broke over her, he caught her cry against his devouring kiss and thrust his finger deeper. That strong pulse of her pleasure clutching him, anointing his finger with that hot, sweet liquid balm.

So damn good. Only one thing could be better, and he was working slowly, steadily toward it. Taking his time.

She stirred and looked up at him. “Wow,” she whispered.

“Yeah,” he muttered, his voice hoarse. His body shook with need. “In my fantasies, I made you come over and over. Multiple times, until you were so primed and ready, you were begging me to have my way with you.”

She shook with silent giggles. “Begging? Really?”

“Oh, give me a break,” he protested. “It was a horny bad-boy fantasy, okay?”

“I’m not complaining,” she teased. “I’m so hot and bothered. Lay it on me. So what happened next in the fantasy? What did I beg you for? Be really, ah…specific.”

Zack tagged the silky pajama bottoms off her hips, along with her panties. They pooled around her feet, and she kicked them away. Her eyes were dilated, locked with his in the illuminated mirror. Her lips were hot red, shadows painting her perfect naked body so sharp and bold. Every detail illuminated as he ran his hands over her sweet curves.

Zack seized her hips, tugging them back so she caught herself on the edge of the vanity for balance. He shoved down his own sweatpants, freeing his stiff, aching erection.

Ava licked her lips, making them gleam. That hot, luscious pink that made his body clench and pulse with need. Her eyes, demanding everything he had to give her.

They were breathlessly silent. No need for words as

he caressed the shadowy heat between her legs, opening her. Pressing himself inside, and then a slow, deep shove—

The vanity banged and rattled against the wall. A perfume bottle fell over with a tinkling clatter. They froze in dismay.

"Oh, crap," Ava whispered.

They held their breath in the silence, but no one called out.

"I think Drew and Jenna and Vann and Sophie are too busy in bed themselves to be bothered about us, thank God." Zack seized her hands and splayed them against the wall on either side of the narrow mirror. "I like the mirror," he said. "Looking at us makes me crazy. I can't give that up. Just don't touch the vanity. We won't make a sound."

Ava responded with a siren smile, arching her body sensually, hands braced against the wall, pushing back to take more of him. "Is this the part where I beg you?" she whispered. "Oh, please, Zack. Please. Do it. Give it all to me. I want it so bad."

Whoa. He almost lost it right then but hung on to his control.

He thrust inside her again, moving slowly and carefully until they found their rhythm. Once they did, it almost impossible to stay quiet. To not groan and bang and shout. Ava couldn't control the panting whimpers that jerked out of her at every slick, heavy stroke. He loved the jolt and sway of her perfect breasts, the way she caught her luscious lower lip between her teeth. It all drove him crazy. Spurred him onward.

At the end, he felt her orgasm crashing through her.

The power seized him and he gave in to it, forgetting everything but their bodies, moving, melding. The wrenching throb of her pleasure drawing out his own until his climax exploded. Wiping him out.

He had no idea if he had made a racket. It was anyone's guess.

But amazingly, the house's silence held. He pulled Ava upright and held her against him. She trembled, damp with a sheen of sweat. "Are you cold?" he asked.

"Give me a sec." She pulled away and disappeared into a connecting bathroom.

Zack pulled his sweatpants back on and sat down on Ava's bed to wait. It seemed presumptuous to get into her bed, not knowing if she wanted him to sleep there with Drew next door and Malcolm right down the hall.

The bathroom door opened. Ava emerged, still gorgeously naked. She strolled over to the bed, stretching and tossing back her hair. Clearly enjoying his gaze on her.

"Should I go back to my room?" he said. "I don't want to risk causing any tension."

She considered that for a moment, and shook her head. "No. Stay. We're not doing anything wrong. And I want you. Right here."

He let out a slow, relieved breath. *Oh, thank God.*

"Well?" she said. "Pull down the covers, you horny, opportunistic bad boy, you. Let's get comfy."

He did as she asked and stretched out on her bed. Ava leaned over to him for a kiss, letting her hair brush the length of his torso like a long, delicately stimulating kiss.

"So, Zack," she said. "You know all those hot fantasies of yours?"

"What about them?" he asked warily.

"Well, you should know… I had my own corresponding fantasies. From the day of that barbecue and onward. I didn't sleep that night, either. I just lay there and I thought about you. I thought about you so hard. And I did things. You know. To myself."

"Oh my God," he whispered. "Tell me more. Or you could show me, too."

"Yeah? Would you like that?" She slid lower, trailing her fingers down the treasure trail of hair on his belly, toward his newly stiffened penis.

"Oh, yeah," he muttered.

"My fantasies were even naughtier than yours," she whispered. "Want to see?"

Zack shuddered with helpless excitement. "Yes, please," he said hoarsely.

Sixteen

Zack woke up with Ava wrapped in his arms, his legs tangled with hers. He lay there for a moment just enjoying the heat and the closeness. He watched her face as her eyes fluttered open, and she smiled at him, stretching luxuriously. A good sign.

"Hey there, you," he said. "How's the tide line today?"

She thought about it. "Pretty good." Her husky, sleep-roughened voice had a smile in it. "Which is a miracle when I wake up in this house."

He grinned at her. "Music to my ears."

"I'm grabbing a shower," she said. "So you'd better sneak on back to your room. I don't want to be stark naked when I have this conversation with Drew or my uncle."

"Fair enough," he said. "I think I might lurk in here awhile longer, though. I hear some activity out there. People stumbling out of their rooms, looking for coffee."

"When I'm out, I'll do recon," she said. "You can go back when the coast is clear."

"Or we could just stay in bed for a while longer," he suggested hopefully. "We could kill some time. Until they're all downstairs having brunch. Could be fun."

"Ha. Nice try, buddy. It was kinky enough last night when we hoped they were all asleep. You be good."

"Oh, always."

She was giggling as she got into the shower. A good omen. He grabbed his athletic pants from the floor, unzipped the pocket and pulled out the ring box.

Balls out. When she came out of the shower, he was laying it on the line.

He was about to toss the blanket off his naked self when the room door flew open and Jenna burst in, in her bathrobe, a towel wrapped around her head. "Av, would you lend me some… Oh, holy shit!" Jenna jerked backward in shock, mouth open.

"Morning, Jenna," he said evenly.

Ava emerged from bathroom wrapped in a towel, gasping when she saw her friend.

"Yikes," she squeaked. "And so it begins. Hey, Jenn. Did you sleep well?"

"Uh…sure. I… I guess." Jenna gaped at him, then at Ava. "Damn. I'm so sorry."

"Close the door, at least," Ava told her. "Since we're both naked."

"Oh, of course." Jenna did so, her gaze skittering away from Zack's bare torso.

Zack's fingers closed around the velvet ring box. He slid it back into the pocket of the pants, still under the cover of the duvet. So it was not ordained that this business be wrapped up before breakfast. The moment has been well and truly burned.

"I am so sorry," Jenna said. "I just never… I mean, I heard the shower running from the other side of the wall, so I knew you were up, so I thought I'd just pop in and knock on the bathroom door, you know, and ask if you had some old leggings I could borrow. Because all of a sudden, my jeans are too tight. From one day to the next."

"Sure thing." Ava pulled open a drawer of her bureau. "Color preference? Black, gray, dark blue, dark red?"

"Black is fine," Jenna said.

"There you go." Ava tossed them, and Jenna caught them one-handed.

"So, um…why did I not hear of this?" Jenna asked her. "Why the secrecy?"

"You've been out of the country for weeks, Jenn," Ava reminded her. "It's not secret. Just really new."

"I should've guessed after last night," Jenna said. "All those weird vibes pinging around the room. It gave me a weird, tingly feeling. And now I know why."

Ava smiled at her. "Good vibes, mostly. So? See you at breakfast?"

"Oh. Yeah. Of course. So sorry. Really. I'm out of here."

The door clicked shut after Jenna. Zack gave Ava a what-do-you-want-from-me shrug. "Cat's out of the bag."

"Don't you dare sound smug about it," Ava warned him. "You're not the one who'll have Uncle Malcolm breathing down your neck like a dragon."

"You don't think so? Let's go downstairs and find out."

"Sure," Ava said, pulling on her clothes. "I'll go down first. You get a shower and straggle in after a decent interval."

He did as Ava commanded and was the last person to join the brunch table.

Mrs. Alvarez had laid out a spectacular buffet, and he was grateful for it. A night like that generated a hell of an appetite. There was strong coffee, fresh-squeezed orange juice, a cheesy breakfast casserole, grilled bacon and sausages, smoked salmon and cream cheese with bagels, and freshly baked lemon scones, still steaming from the oven.

Conversation suddenly ceased when he walked in. Zack loaded up his plate and took the place next to Ava. What the hell. Might as well start as he meant to go on.

Drew and Jenna exchanged meaningful glances. Vann and Drew did the same. Then Sophie and Vann. Sophie and Jenna stifled their giggles with coughing fits.

Then the silence was broken only by the clink of his coffee spoon.

Malcolm stared around at all of them, eyes slitted and suspicious. "What in the hell is going on here?" he demanded. "What are you kids all chortling about? Spit it out!"

No one said a word. Ava placed her cup down in the saucer with a rattle.

To hell with this. Zack put down his fork and placed his hand over Ava's on the table. He clasped her fingers, lifted her hand and pressed a slow kiss against her knuckles. A silent declaration of intent.

Ava gave him a startled look.

"Let's do this," he said to her. "I can't stand the suspense any longer."

"What the hell is this?" Malcolm barked. "What have you been doing behind my back?"

"It's not behind your back," Zack told him. "It's right front and center."

"Don't you give me any sass," Malcolm snarled. He turned his glower upon Ava. "Just what do you have to say for yourself, young lady?"

Ava sighed. "I'm not a young lady," she said. "I am an adult woman. Zack and I really connected down at the trade show in LA. We're really enjoying each other's company and seeing where it goes."

"And I assume that last night, it went straight into your childhood bedroom?"

"That is none of your business," Ava said coolly.

"The hell it's not!" Malcolm turned on Zack, his eyes popping. "You opportunistic bastard! I thought it was fishy, dropping everything to run down to LA with her. Not so altruistic after all, eh? Was that your plan all along? Get close to her and seduce her?"

"That's offensive and ridiculous," Ava snapped. "Control yourself, Uncle. You're being a bully."

"No, he's right," Zack said.

Ava froze and turned to stare at him. "What?"

"What exactly do you mean by that?" Drew's voice was suddenly hard.

"Malcolm's right," Zack told them. "It was a golden opportunity to do what I've wanted to do for years." His hand tightening around Ava's. "I've wanted you since the moment I laid eyes on you," he said to her. "Like I told you last night. I saw my chance to get close to you, and I took it. And I'll fight anyone or anything to stay close to you." He looked around the table. "For the rest of my life. So you all know where I stand."

"Zack!" Ava hissed. "For God's sake! Cool it!"

"I can't," he said. "I care too much."

The silence was broken by a sniffle across the table. "Aw," Jenna said, her eyes wet. "That's beautiful, Zack. God, I'm so emotional right now. Gets me in the feels."

"Absolutely. Me, too." Sophie dabbed at her eyes with her napkin and reached across Vann's plate to pat Zack's hand. "May true love prevail. Always."

"For God's sake, spare me." Uncle Malcolm shoved back from the table, hard enough to rattle the plates and jiggle the cups in their saucers. "Finding out that my houseguest debauched my niece under my own roof puts me off my breakfast. Be ready to catch the ferry this evening, all of you. No one bother me until then!"

He grabbed his cane and stomped out of the room, muttering darkly.

Ava covered her face with her hand. "Ouch," she whispered. "That went well."

"He's just wound up," Jenna soothed her. "Don't worry. He's still jet-lagged, and there's been so much stress and change the last few months. But he'll come around."

Drew grunted. "He's never handled stress or change well. Not even when he was younger. He's not likely to improve now."

Jenna frowned at him and gave Ava a hug from behind, kissing the top of her head. "Don't listen to him, babe," she said. "Come upstairs and let me show you the dresses I have to choose from for tonight. You, too, Sophie. And tell us everything."

Ava gave Zack a speaking glance as she rose from the chair and allowed herself to be pulled out of the room by her friend and her newfound cousin. The men listened to the sound of the women's voices retreating up the stairs.

Then Drew shoved his chair back, slouching in his chair, and looked Zack straight in the eye. "So let me get this straight," he said. "You've lusted after my little sister for the last ten years. Then you found out that she had a serious security issue. And while she was feeling attacked and vulnerable, while the rest of her family was out of the country, with no clue that all this was going on, you swept in on your white charger to be her sole rescuer. And took the opportunity to travel out of town with her. To hover over her 24-7. And finally, to seduce her. Wow, Zack. What a prince of a guy. I'm impressed."

"That's not exactly how I would describe what happened," Zack said.

"Yeah?" Drew crossed his arms over his chest, one of Malcolm's gestures. "Tell me how it really was, then. After all, we have all the time in the world. We have hours to discuss this situation. All day, in fact. Have at, buddy. I'm all ears."

Zack drained his coffee, steeling himself against his friend's cold anger.

No way out of this but through.

Seventeen

"Try not to worry about them, honey," Jenna urged her. "Wilbur and Bobby are not quite as helpless as they let you think they are. They like it when you do the heavy lifting, but they know it's not in their best interests to play dumb. They'll keep their act together."

"I suppose you're right," Ava replied, but she kept an anxious eye the Blooms, who were talking with her brother across the grand ballroom. The tuxedos she and Ernest had found fit pretty well, considering. It had been no easy feat to find them, as the Blooms were six foot three and skeletally thin. But they looked quite respectable and like they were enjoying themselves. So far, so good.

"I'm glad you went with the red dress," Sophie told her. "Zack couldn't take his eyes off you."

Ava smiled at her. "It fits the theme. Being the scarlet woman of the hour."

"Don't worry about that," Jenna urged. "Malcolm has already started to calm down. He just has to make room for the idea in his head. At his age, that takes time."

"Agreed," Sophie said. "He even laughed at Vann's jokes on the ferry."

"He may laugh and smile with you guys, but when it comes to Uncle Malcolm, I'm afraid my mileage may vary," Ava said ruefully.

Ava watched Jenna and Sophie exchange meaningful glances. She didn't wonder that Malcolm was glad to have the two of them around. His new niece-in-law and newfound daughter were wonderful additions to the family—bright, passionate and accomplished, and they both looked stunning tonight, Jenna in an empire waist gown beaded with silver and gold beads, and Sophie in a glittering, metallic bronze halter dress that clung lovingly to her lush, elegant body, leaving her tanned back completely bare.

Things were still tense for her and Zack, but Drew had calmed down. He and Zack had evidently thrashed it out after breakfast, although Zack was unwilling to tell her about that conversation. She got the sense of an uneasy truce. Weird, tense undercurrents.

Then she felt the hairs on the back of her neck prickle up. A low, excited ripple of conversation. Someone caught her eye and looked swiftly away. Then another. The hell?

Suddenly, people were quickly making way for Trevor Wexford, who was charging across the room toward her. And he looked pissed.

"What do those idiots think they're doing?" Trevor

demanded. "That absentminded genius bullshit will only go so far. I don't buy it anymore."

"What on earth are you talking about?" Ava demanded, bewildered.

Trevor held up his phone. "This is from the Blooms' social media accounts!"

Ava focused on the screen and gasped. Trevor helpfully swiped up, making the images scroll. They were horribly familiar. Callista's head, clumsily photoshopped over naked bodies or dressed in dominatrix garb. Banner captions about frauds, sluts, skanks.

"It's not the Blooms," she said swiftly. "I swear it. They've been hacked."

"Then fix it! Make it stop! Or I will end them, and you! Do you understand me?"

"Certainly. Calm down, Trevor. I swear, this is not Bobby or Wilbur's—"

"Prove it!"

"I will. Just give me a little time." Ava glanced wildly around for backup.

Sophie was right behind her, already talking into her phone in a businesslike voice. "…to interrupt your Saturday evening, but this is life or death, Mindy. Get the whole team moving. We have to find out who hacked the Blooms right away. Get back to me the instant you have news. Thanks." She closed the call. "My cybersecurity team is on it, Mr. Wexford. They're the best in the business."

"They'd better be." He gave them a dark look and strode away.

Ava gave Sophie a grateful glance. "Thanks. I have

to find Wilbur and Bobby, quick. They'd better find out about this from me."

Then she spotted them hurrying toward her. Too late. As she watched, Wilbur tripped over his feet, and Bobby knocked a glass of champagne from the hands of a portly matron, splashing it over her ample bosom. He compounded his gaffe by grabbing a napkin from a table and trying to sponge the lady's cleavage off himself.

Ava grabbed Bobby's arm and towed him away from the sputtering lady. "Sorry, Mrs. Winthrop!" she called out as she dragged the two out of the ballroom, into the stairwell and swiftly down a flight of stairs, out of harm's way. "What the hell, guys?"

"Someone's trying to ruin us!" Bobby moaned. "Ernest told us about the hack! Someone is trolling Callista and making it look like it's us!"

Damn. She was going to kill that graceless clod Ernest for getting them agitated. "Calm down, Bobby," she soothed. "We'll fix this."

"But that smut is all over Callista Wexford's socials!" Wilbur gnawed his nails, blinking frantically. "We should never have come here! This kind of place just gives the haters a chance to mess with us."

"Wrong attitude, boys," Ava said bracingly. "We fight back. Sophie's team is working on it. They'll see that it's not you two. You two just lie low here for a few minutes while I run and find Zack. I want his take on this. Just chill."

She couldn't help thinking, as she ran back upstairs, how much had changed in the past week. Tough, independent Ava, running off to her new boyfriend for help, like a little kid with a skinned knee who wanted her owie fussed over.

But having a smart, fiercely competent, protective security expert for a boyfriend was a luxury. She was damn well going to take advantage of it.

She loved having Zack at her side when things got scary.

Eighteen

There they went again. Zack caught the eye of another guy in a group nearby, saw his gaze flick away and then heard a burst of smothered laughter. Not for the first time.

He forced himself to focus in on what Drew was saying about his conversation with the Bloom brothers. "...the Beyond Earth project," Drew was saying. "Ava's right. The work they're doing is the missing link that could make the program viable. I hope we can pin them down for talks now that they're the flavor of the month."

Again. Another nervous snort of laughter. "What's with those bozos?" he snarled.

"Who?" Drew looked back over his shoulder, but the clot of people had dispersed.

"Never mind. People giving me the side-eye. I started noticing it a few minutes ago."

Drew's eyebrows climbed. "Guilty conscience, after spending the night rolling around in my sister's bed?"

"No guilt," Zack said. "Not even a little."

"Come on, Drew," Vann said wearily. "I thought we put this to bed. Let's not get wound up again out here in full public view."

"Better yet," Zack said. "I'll just go find my girlfriend, if you'll excuse me. I'm ready for some civil, reasonable conversation."

He strode away and was halfway across the crowded ballroom when it occurred to him that maybe Drew was right and he was hypersensitive. Who wouldn't be, after a long day of massive, relentless ball breaking from the overprotective, wiseass older brother? Damn.

"Zack! Thank God you're here!"

He spun around. It was Ernest, his white-blond hair sticking up like he'd been electrified. "What is it?" he demanded. "Is Ava okay?"

"She's fine, but we have a problem! I wanted to give you a heads-up, because—"

"Zack! Did you know?" A loud, penetrating female voice behind him.

He turned to see Callista Wexford striking a dramatic pose in the door to the room, clad in skintight black velvet. Lots of draped diamonds, bosom way out to there, but this was no time to contemplate the marvels of nature. She looked like she wanted to tear his head off. "Excuse me?" he asked. "Know what?"

"This!" she shrilled, holding up her phone.

Zack leaned forward, wincing at the ugly images. "Oh, no. Damn it."

"Can you believe this?" Callista's strident voice drew

attention from all sides. "Trevor offered those two lunatics everything they could ever dream of, and this is the thanks they give us?"

"The Blooms are not responsible," he said.

"But it's coming from them! They're generating it all!"

"Bobby and Wilbur would never do this, even if they had the actual capability, which I doubt they do," Zack said. "I'd be surprised if those two even know how social media platforms work. Let's find out who runs their accounts first, and then we can start pointing fingers at—"

"Ava," Ernest said.

Zack turned to him, bewildered. "The hell?"

"Ava runs their social media accounts," Ernest clarified helpfully. "You're right about the Blooms. Those two don't have the first clue about any of it. Ava set all those accounts up for them years ago. She runs it all for them."

Callista's eyes widened. "Ah! I'm starting to get it. Ava got jealous down in LA, right? When I chatted you up at the trade show? She wants to show me who's boss. That conniving little slut really thinks she can survive a catfight with me?"

"No way," Zack said hastily. "Absolutely not. I'm sure she'd never—"

"Don't even try defending her," Callista hissed. "I hope you see what that woman is made of before you hurt yourself. Fair warning, Zack. I'm taking Ava Maddox down in a big, public way. So back away slowly if you don't want to crash with her."

Callista spun around and marched away, her heels clicking angrily.

Zack turned to Ernest. "I've got to find Ava, quickly."

"I think I saw her run upstairs," Ernest said. "Up toward the Blazon office."

"Thanks." Zack ignored the glances and murmuring as he wove through the throng. He raced up one flight of the big, spiraling Gilded Age staircase.

He stopped to look for her in the library, just in case, striding swiftly through a dark-paneled room lined with books, between leather sofas and reading tables. No Ava.

He made his way back toward the stairwell, but stopped when Vikram came through the doorway. His face was grim, and his dark eyes looked worried.

"Zack," he said. "I'm glad I caught you."

"Can't talk now, Vikram. I'm trying to find Ava. We have a serious problem."

"I know. That's what I need to discuss with you."

Something about Vikram's tone gave Zack a twinge of dread. "What is it?"

"Um…damn, Zack. I don't know how to say this. It's really embarrassing—"

"Just say it. Please."

Vikram's face tightened. "Okay, here goes." He pulled out his smartphone and tapped on it. "One of the guys on Ava's team of bodyguards found this online. It was posted a couple of hours ago." He set the video clip to play, and handed the phone to Zack.

Zack held the device gingerly, as if it might blow up in his hand. The link was titled The First Kiss… Part 1: Her Bad Boy Bodyguard!

It was Ava's hotel room in Los Angeles, and the camera was directed at the bed. Suddenly Zack appeared in the camera's field, carrying Ava, still in her gray cami and boy shorts. Her legs were wrapped around his waist. He sat down on the bed and dragged her closer, letting her hair tumble around his face as she straddled him, moving against his body, starting to kiss him.

The video cut off. A pop-up appeared on the menu.

You like? Lots more coming! Like and share! Part Two coming soon!

Vikram reached out, gently taking his phone back out of Zack's numb hand.

"I can see from your face that this is a surprise," he said.

"Yes," Zack forced out.

"Okay. I was afraid that… I mean, I didn't know if maybe the two of you had recorded that for fun, or—"

"Fun?" His voice was getting louder. "For *fun?*"

Vikram put both his hands up. "No judgment if you did, right? Lots of people use video for their—"

"I do not use video." He bit the words out one by one."

"Don't get pissed at me," Vikram said swiftly. "I'm just the messenger."

Zack shook his head. "I'm not. I'm just… I don't understand how this could have happened."

"Well, um. About that." Vikram gulped. "Given the situation that's come up with Callista Wexford, it really, you know, makes you wonder, right?"

"Wonder what?" Zack's voice got harder.

"Well, the video is already going viral. And just look how Ava Maddox and Blazon have been trending since it posted."

Zack shook his head. "No."

Vikram shrank from the rage in Zack's eyes. "Sorry. I just had to get it out there. It's what she does, Zack. Attention, buzz, likes, follows, eyeballs, that's her stock in trade. It's very telling that it appears right when the thing with Callista breaks."

"You're wrong," Zack said. "She would never hurt the Blooms. She loves those guys. Watch what you say, Vikram."

Vikram took a careful step back "I'm sorry," he said stiffly. "I shouldn't have said anything. I thought I was doing my job. Telling you what I saw, and what I really think. Even if it's hard to hear."

"I'm not mad at you," Zack said. "I appreciate the info, and your candor. But let's let this go for now. We'll talk more later."

Vikram backed away out the door, looking relieved.

Zack stood there, trying to square reality with the volcanic buildup of rage inside him. *Bad boy bodyguard?* He pulled out his phone, pulled up the platform Vikram had been using and entered the title into the search bar.

Sure enough. Three thousand and seventy views already. It was only a fragment of their encounter, twenty-five seconds of video, but there was no reason to think that hours more had not been recorded. Hours of wild sex, starring him and Ava, out there for the world to watch and know about. His friends, colleagues, bosses. His sister. His mother.

The door opened, and Ava burst through, talking on her phone. Her eyes lit up as she saw him, but she kept talking. "No, I can't yet. I just found him in the library, so don't worry about it… Just wait for me there, okay? I know it's an emergency. I'll be up there as soon as I can. I have to talk to Zack before I…yes. Fine. Later."

She ended the call and hurried toward him. "I'm so glad you're here!" Her voice was a breathless rush. "We have a problem. The Blooms just got hacked, like me."

"Did they?" he asked.

Her perfectly shaped brown eyebrows tilted up, puzzled at his tone. "Yes! And to my eye, it has the same style and vibe as whoever was trashing me."

"I see." His voice sounded dead to his own ears.

He had to sharpen up. Tease the facts from the fiction. Or rather, to tease facts out of his own romantic fantasies.

No matter what it cost him.

Something was very wrong.

Ava stopped short on her rush toward him. "Zack?" she asked. "Are you okay?"

"No," he said. "Not even close."

"Why are you looking at me like that?" she asked. "I was hoping you'd help me get ahead of this problem. Which you seem to already be aware of. Somehow."

"Ava," he said. "Just tell me what you know about this." Zack lifted his phone so she could see the screen.

The video was already playing. Ava stared at it in disbelief. Her phone slid out of her hand and thudded to the carpet at her feet.

The video clip stopped. The frozen still image was of her, cupping Zack's face as she came in for a kiss.

"That was filmed from your laptop in LA," he said. "The camera was on the desk."

She gazed at him, horrified. "You can't possibly think that I filmed that on purpose," she whispered. "Good God, Zack. Why would I?"

"I don't know. But no one knew that encounter was going to happen, Ava. God, not even me. How could someone else have possibly set us up?"

"You think that I'd make a…a sex tape?" Her voice cracked. "And post it online, for everyone to see? That's my worst nightmare! Why would I do that?"

"I don't know," Zack said. "I don't get it, either."

"I have never lied to you!" she said, her voice impassioned. "I've been more honest and real with you than I've ever been with anyone in my whole life!"

"Then explain this." He gestured with his phone. "What is this? Who could have done it, if not you?"

"I don't know," she said, her voice small. "I've got nothing."

But she could see that it was no use. He had that look on his face. A brick wall. Confusion, suspicion. And so much anger.

She backed away. "I think we're done here."

"I'll call a bodyguard to escort you home," Zack said.

"No, I think not. My security is my own concern from now on. Don't trouble yourself." She pulled her stole around herself, turned and ran.

People tried to talk to her as she stumbled down the stairway. She heard her name called. Saw Sophie, with a frown of concern in her eye. Drew's worried look across the ballroom. Thank God they were too far away to stop her as she hurried down the broad marble staircase toward the front door.

Seattle drizzle was soothing against her hot face and bare shoulders as she lurched down the street, hiking the skirt up into her hands.

She knew this sick falling feeling from her plane crash nightmares. When the plane was already caught in the relentless grip of gravity and was hurtling down, down, down.

Braced for impact.

Nineteen

Zack remembered this feeling from missions in the Anbar Province that had gone sideways. Bad intel, an unknown, unassessed threat flicking past the corner of his eye and mind. Unknown variables; nudging at his senses, but not nudging quite hard enough.

The hell? Someone had just planted a bomb right inside the most important part of his life. He'd already detonated it and *now* he was questioning the intel?

Of course he was questioning it. He was head over ass in love with that woman.

"…hear me, Zack? Hey! Earth to Zack!"

His gaze whipped around. Sophie was in the doorway, phone in hand.

"What?" he asked.

"We just saw Ava running off like her hair was on fire. What upset her?"

"Me," he admitted.

Sophie's mouth tightened. "Can you go after her and fix it?"

"I don't think it's fixable," he said.

"But she—" Sophie's phone rang again, and she picked it up. "Mindy? What have you got?" She listened for a moment. "Whoa. I'll go check it out right away. Call you right back." Sophie closed the call. "The latest attack against Callista Wexford originated from Blazon's IP address. Ava's own company, right here in the Gilchrist building. In real time. Whoever's doing it is there right now and isn't making the faintest attempt to mask it this time. Call Ava right now, and tell her to get back to the building. Let's all just go upstairs and see who it is."

If his guts could have dropped lower, they would have. "What do you mean, back in the building? Ava's right here."

"No, she is not. I saw her run out the door myself! Look out the window, and you'll still see her on the street. In that dress you could see her from space."

Zack leaned to look out the window. He caught sight of her instantly. The wind tunnel of tall buildings made her skirt billow out. Her updo had tumbled down, curls trailing over her bare back. Her stole fluttered behind her like a battle flag.

She wasn't involved in this. She wasn't upstairs, at Blazon. She wasn't even holding her phone.

The feeling that gripped him was a strange mix of horror, relief and guilt, but he had no time for feelings. Sophie joined him at the window and made a worried sound when she spotted Ava. She lifted her phone.

"This has to be dealt with fast," she said, pulling up the number.

Ava's rock-and-roll ringtone started to play, right in the room. "Oh, no." Sophie bent to pick up Ava's phone and looked up at him. "I'm guessing that you might have jumped to some really dumb conclusions, Zack," she said.

"Scold me later." Zack was already in motion. "I'm going up to Blazon."

His feet flew up the stairs to the top floor. It was quiet and deserted up there. He sprinted down to the end of the hall, the last two doors, with the sign that read Blazon Public Relations & Branding Specialists. The frenetic clack of a keyboard came from inside. Zack flung the door open.

Ernest was hunched over the keyboard. He jerked around with a startled squeak, eyes bugged, his mouth a big O. He spun around, hit a few keys and then sprinted hell for leather toward the emergency exit stairway.

Zack gave chase, catching him by the collar of his shirt just as he hit the panic bar of the door and reeling him back. "Hold it right there, Ernest."

"Let go of me! Let go! You're choking me!"

"Nope. I'm not letting go of you. What are you doing here?"

"Just some work I forgot about," Ernest said, his voice an aggrieved whine. "I just thought I'd pop up here and take care of it, and I'd be able to relax more tomorrow. You scared me to death."

Zack looked at the computer, which was now just a blank blue screen. "Trying to cover your tracks? Too late for that."

"Cover what?" Ernest wiggled in his grasp. "Dude, are you paranoid?"

"You were posting that garbage about Callista," Zack said. "No one else was up here. Ava's outside the building. Tell me what you've been up to. Or else."

Ernest licked his lips, blinking frantically. Zack just waited, letting the seconds tick by. Never easing the pressure on Ernest's shirt collar. Giving the younger man his best wrath-of-God stare.

It worked. Ernest went limp in his grasp, and his mouth started to shake. "Goddamn it," he said shakily. "You asshole. You ruined it. You ruined everything."

"Ruined what?" Zack demanded.

"Ava was supposed to come up here first, not you!"

Ernest started to sob. Zack had a disorienting moment of total, awful comprehension. Puzzle pieces clicked into place. He was a goddamn fool for not seeing it.

"Ava was on the phone with you when she came to the library to talk to me," he said slowly. "You were trying to lure her up so that I would find her here, after the team saw the posts about Callista coming straight from this IP address. You meant for me and Sophie's team to catch her red-handed. Or better yet, for Callista and Trevor to find her."

"You screwed it all up!" Ernest wailed.

"Guilty as charged." He pushed Ernest down onto the office chair and, with a shove, sent it rolling back to hit the wall. He advanced on Ernest. "Now tell me why."

"Let me go!" Ernest tried to stand up. Zack blocked him, and he dropped back into the chair, sniveling.

"No one's going to save you, Ernest," Zack said. "Talk fast."

"She deserved it!" Ernest burst out. "She got my brother thrown in prison! She got that lying, whining hag out of jail! None of that stuff she said about Colby is true! I know Colby didn't do that! I know Colby! He wouldn't do that!"

"Colby? Wait…are you talking about Colby Hoyt?" Zack asked. "You're Colby Hoyt's brother? But your last name isn't Hoyt."

"Different mom." Ernest sniffled loudly. "I'm eight years younger than him. Our dad never married my mom. His name wasn't on my documents. But Colby's still my brother. I can't just do nothing! He was up for parole a year ago, and she just pushed her goddamn lying bullshit video again and killed that, too! I had to do something for him!"

Zack thought back to the conversation he'd had with Ava that first night. He remembered seeing Colby Hoyt on the news. He'd had the same washed-out coloring as Ernest. The white-blond hair, the near-invisible brows and lashes, the oversize, droopy eyes. But Colby had seemed meaner and harder.

"You're getting back at Ava for helping Judy Whelan get out of jail and helping to convict your brother," Zack said, his voice stony. "So that's what this is about."

"She deserved it!" Ernest's voice was thick with trapped snot. "She just decides what the story is and makes one of her goddamn documentaries and it all looks so convincing. But it's a bunch of lies!"

He wanted to pound this little punk so badly, but he just breathed it out, slow and even. "So this is your punishment? Trashing her rep? Sex tapes? Hurting the Blooms?"

"It's just a game for her. But I can play that game, too. I used her own tricks against her. I want the world to know that she's a liar and a cheat. And a slut."

"She would have helped you," Zack said. "She believed in you. She would have helped you launch a brilliant career in marketing. But you flushed it all down the toilet for someone else's spite. Bad move, Ernest."

Ernest started to cry. "I had no choice!" he blubbered. "Colby's my brother. He asked me to—"

"Don't care," Zack said. "Not interested. Save it for your lawyer. Just one last thing before I call the cops. Did you post the rest of that video?"

"Only the teaser so far," Ernest admitted. "But I edited and uploaded the next installment. It's, like, two and a half hours of material, once you edit out the breaks and talking and naps. All I have to do is hit the go button." His eyes went crafty. "Maybe we can work out a deal? Say, I take that recording down, and you, like, um…let me go?"

"I'll tell you our deal," Zack said. "Take the recording down. Delete it while I watch. And maybe, just maybe, I won't break all your bones while we wait for the police. That's your prize. A functional skeleton. Do we understand each other?"

Ernest's face crumpled. "But I did it for Colby," he sobbed.

The police came, in due course. The hours ground by. All Zack wanted to do was to go after Ava, but instead, he was stuck there, following through on all the time-eating bureaucratic protocols that were put in motion when the police were summoned.

Then Ava's people piled on, demanding explanations. Sophie and Vann and Drew showed up, and then Malcolm stormed in with Bev and Hendrick, demanding to be debriefed.

The one bright spot was when Jenna called to confirm that Ava had gotten home safely. Ava was not, however, answering her phone, which Jenna had since returned to her. His calls went to voice mail. His texts were left unread. She was freezing him out.

He damn well deserved it. And it made him frantic.

She wouldn't answer Malcolm or Drew's calls, either, which prompted them to go check on her in person. Delaying still further the time he could go to her house himself.

Drew stopped halfway out the door and gazed back at Zack, his eyes troubled. "I gave you a really hard time today," he said. "But it's my job. You have a sister yourself, so I know you understand. Even so, thanks for watching her back. And for catching the troll. I just wanted to say good luck. With Ava, I mean."

Zack's jaw ached. "I'll need it," he said. "Ernest had me fooled for a few minutes, and Ava saw it. She feels betrayed. It's a bad scene."

"So fix it," Drew said forcefully. "Find a way. I haven't seen her as happy as she was today since before my parents' plane crash. I want her to have that. So make it work, bro. Figure it out."

Zack nodded. He didn't need to be told what was at stake.

Not to be outdone, Malcolm stepped forward and

stared down at Zack from under his bushy white brows, his arms folded over his chest. He harrumphed. “You do know, of course, that if you hurt her, I’ll rip your head off and use it for a bowling ball.”

Zack suppressed the urge to laugh just in time. “I doubt it will come to that, sir.”

When he was finally free to go, he drove straight to Ava’s house and parked down the block, waiting until her family members came out and drove away.

When the cars had all gone, he walked up to her door, gazed up into the security camera he’d had installed and hit the buzzer.

Praying for mercy.

Twenty

Ava shivered as she stared at the security monitor on the wall by the door. This was all she needed, after all those hours on the phone trying to fix this godawful mess. The Blooms, the Wexfords, Uncle Malcolm, Drew, Sophie, the police. She was exhausted, but at this point, it seemed like everyone knew the score.

Everyone but her and Zack. That was still up in the air.

Zack gazed up into her eyes through the camera with that look he got when he was holding his heart wide-open. She wasn't pressing the intercom, so she didn't hear him, but saw his lips form the word. *Please.*

Damn the man. So the torture wasn't even over for the day. This was the final act.

She hit the intercom. "Zack, go home. I'm fine. Let's get some sleep."

"Please let me in," he said.

She'd given him keys, but he didn't use them. Because of course he wouldn't. He was an old-fashioned, righteous dude whose mama and granddad had brought him up right.

"My family just left," she said into the intercom. "They already wore me out."

"I know. I saw them go. I've been parked down the block, waiting."

"Oh. Well, I'm exhausted, and I've got nothing left for you. Besides, truthfully, Zack? There isn't anything left to say."

"There's everything to say," Zack said. "Please, open the door. I know I don't deserve it. But I'm ready to grovel."

That gave her pause. "Grovel? Really? Zack Austin, the great and powerful?"

"If groveling is what you need from me, I'll do it. Just let me in."

She hesitated, unwilling to unleash any fresh pain and turmoil. Besides, she hadn't taken off the makeup that had run under her eyes, or even bothered to comb her wind-snarled hair. She'd just pulled the tangled mess back into a scrunchie to deal with later.

She picked the simplest, lamest excuse. "I look like crap. We'll talk later, Zack."

"You know damn well I think you're the most beautiful woman I've ever seen. Just five minutes. Then I swear, I'll go."

She cursed under her breath, blew out a sharp breath and jerked the door open.

She stood there in her entry hall, swathed in her big,

puffy, dark crimson fleece bathrobe. Bare feet sticking out, swollen and sore from the long, lonely walk in high heels before Jenna found her. Jenna had called a car, driven around in it until she spotted Ava, and given her a ride home. Saint Jenna.

Zack stepped inside and closed the door. He lifted up his open palm, which held the keys to the two new locks now on her door. The copies she'd given him when they got back from Los Angeles.

"These are yours," he said. "Having these keys means more to me than anything ever has before in my life." He laid them on the shelf by the door. "I hope you'll give them back to me."

Ava dragged her gaze away from the shiny, newly minted keys gleaming on the shelf. "Wow. You are the master of the symbolic gesture, Zack."

His eyes narrowed. "I'm not quite sure what that means tonight."

"Not much, I guess," she said. "I'm babbling. Long day. I need rest."

"With no one guarding you?"

Ava gave him an ironic look. "That's all over now. The threat has passed, and my life can return to normal. Whatever the hell that ever was."

"Ava—"

"It's really depressing and sad that it was Ernest all along, because I cared about that guy, and I tried to mentor him. I thought he was really bright and talented. And all along, he was just plotting to destroy me. Wow, there it is again. My incredibly poor judgment, on full display."

He waved that away. "I still want you covered," he

said. "I can't turn it off just like that. I still want to protect you from anything that could possibly hurt you."

"Even you?" she asked.

He flinched. "Ava, please."

"Don't you 'Ava, please' me. You made your opinion of me clear. All that's left is for me to process the information, and I'd rather do that alone. Just go home."

Zack took a step forward, stopping short when she shrank back. "I got confused tonight, Av," he said. "Ernest really blew smoke in my eyes with that sex tape. And I just, ah…lost it."

She swallowed. "Yes. Ernest filmed us. I should have thought of that. But I trusted him. It just never occurred to me."

"Me either. If I'd been thinking straight, I would have remembered that Ernest was in your room that first night, before I went down to the pool to find you."

"But you weren't thinking straight," she said.

Zack shook his head. "No. I wasn't. Please, Ava. Forgive me."

She considered that for a moment. "Just like that?" she said.

"Take all the time you need," he said. "I'll wait. As long as it takes. Years, even."

He just stood there. It was impossible to meet his eyes. She was already on the edge, and if she looked at him, the tears would well up and she would be done for.

"I got bad intel," he said quietly. "It knocked me on my ass. Hit my weakest spot."

"Oh?" She crossed her arms over her chest, sniffing. "So what is your weakest spot, Zack? I should have that info, I guess. Considering what you're asking from me."

He stared at the floor as he considered the question. "My weakest spot," he repeated in a halting voice. "I guess my weakest spot is that I could never quite believe that getting with you was real in the first place. It seemed too good to be true. A woman like you, being into me. Wanting me. That's my weakest spot."

"Oh, Zack—"

"Some part of me was convinced that I didn't deserve it. I was always waiting for the other shoe to drop. So when Vikram showed me the video, suddenly I was there again. That big, dumb lug who got used and played by Aimee in Berlin. The meathead who'd been fooling himself all along. A million miles out of his league, and no freaking clue."

"I see." Her voice was small.

"I came to my senses fast," he went on. "About a minute after you left. Sophie told me about the activity at Blazon's IP address, and I realized what an idiot I was, but I couldn't chase you down. I had to clean up the mess first. With Ernest, and the cops."

Ava nodded, not trusting her voice.

"I never claimed to be perfect, Av." Zack's voice was stark. "I have my weak spots. My dark side. But I love you. I want to spend the rest of my life as close to you as I can get. You're everything to me." His voice broke. He looked down quickly.

It took a while to calm her shaky throat down enough to speak, but she was sure of what she wanted to say once she did. "Okay," she whispered.

Zack's head came up. His fierce gaze fastened onto her. "Okay…to what?"

She held her arms up, open to him. “To this,” she said. “To us.”

They stared at each other. The air between them charged.

“So you forgive me?” he asked slowly.

“I have my dark side, too. And my weak spots.” Her voice was soft but steady and assured. “You made space for them.”

The look on his face echoed the feeling in her own chest. Like light dawning.

“So…we’re good?” he persisted. “Officially?”

She laughed at him, digging a pack of tissues out of her bathrobe pocket and taking a moment to dab at her nose. “Would you please stop it?” she complained. “You’re acting like I’ve got a gun to your head, and it’s weirding me out.”

Zack took the shiny keys off the shelf. He took his keys out of his coat pocket and slowly reattached them to the ring as he moved closer to her.

She laughed at him. “There you go again with your symbolic gestures.”

Zack put his hand into his pocket. “If you liked that symbolic gesture, get a load of this one.” He sank to his knee, lifting a small black velvet box, flipping it open.

Ava gasped. “Oh my God. Zack.”

It was the most stunning ring she’d ever seen. Sensuously coiled strands of multicolored gold, with a big, glowing ruby caught in the center. It was breathtaking.

“I wanted to give you this last night,” Zack said. “We got distracted by our bad-boy fantasies. I tried again this morning, but Jenna walked in. I can’t wait any longer to ask you for the honor of loving and cherishing and protecting you for the rest of my life."

She couldn't speak. Her eyes flooded. Her face shook, like a little earthquake.

"If the ring isn't right, we can change it," he told her. "If you'd prefer a diamond, maybe something more traditional. But I know you like red. I hoped you could wear it with that dress you wore tonight. But your bathrobe looks pretty damn good with it, too."

She shook with a shaky burst of laughter. "It does, actually."

"It was a risky choice," he said. "But that just kind of sum us up, you know? So what the hell. I risked it."

"It's perfect," she whispered, unsteadily. "It's gorgeous. I love it."

"So you'll wear it? You'll risk it?"

"Yes," she said. "Oh, God, yes. For you, I'd risk anything."

Zack slid the ruby ring onto her shaking finger. It fit perfectly. He kissed her cold hand, pressing it to his lips, to his cheek. His hand was shaking as much as hers. He rose to his feet, pulling her into his arms.

"We'll risk it together," he said as their lips met.

* * * * *

Don't miss a single installment in
the Men of Maddox Hill series
by New York Times *bestselling author*
Shannon McKenna!

His Perfect Fake Engagement
Corner Office Secrets
Tall, Dark and Off Limits

Available exclusively
from Harlequin Desire.

COMING NEXT MONTH FROM

HARLEQUIN

DESIRE

#2851 RANCHER'S FORGOTTEN RIVAL

The Carsons of Lone Rock • by Maisey Yates

No one infuriates Juniper Sohappy more than ranch owner Chance Carson. But when Juniper finds him injured and with amnesia on her property, she must help. He believes he's her ranch hand, and unexpected passion flares. But when the truth comes to light, will everything fall apart?

#2852 FROM FEUDING TO FALLING

Texas Cattleman's Club: Fathers and Sons • by Jules Bennett

When Carson Wentworth wins the TCC presidency, tensions flare between him and rival Lana Langley. But to end their familiy feud and secure a fortune for the club, Carson needs her—as his fake fiancée. If they can only ignore the heat between them...

#2853 A SONG OF SECRETS

Hana Trio • by Jayci Lee

After their breakup a decade ago, cellist Angie Han needs composer Jonathan Shin's song to save her family's organization. Striking an uneasy truce, they find their attraction still sizzles. But as their connection grows, will past secrets ruin everything?

#2854 MIDNIGHT SON

Gambling Men • by Barbara Dunlop

Determined to protect his mentor, ruggedly handsome Alaskan businessman Nathaniel Stone is suspicious of the woman claiming to be his boss's long-lost daughter, Sophie Crush. He agrees to get close to her to uncover her intentions, but he cannot ignore their undeniable attraction...

#2855 MILLION-DOLLAR MIX-UP

The Dunn Brothers • by Jessica Lemmon

With her only client MIA, talent agent Kendall Squire travels to his twin's luxe mountain cabin to ask him to fill in. But Max Dunn left Hollywood behind. Now, as they're trapped by a blizzard, things unexpectedly heat up. Has Kendall found her leading man?

#2856 THE PROBLEM WITH PLAYBOYS

Little Black Book of Secrets • by Karen Booth

Publicist Chloe Burnett is a fixer, and sports agent Parker Sullivan needs her to take down a vicious gossip account. She never mixes business with pleasure, but the playboy's hard to resist. When they find themselves in the account's crosshairs, can their relationship survive?

Eve Martin has one goal—find her nephew's father—and her unlikely ally is hotelier Rafael Wentworth, who's just returned to Texas and the family who abandoned him. Soon, she's falling hard for the playboy despite their differences…and their secrets.

Read on for a sneak peek at
The Rebel's Return, *by Nadine Gonzalez.*

"I'm opening a guesthouse in town, similar to this, but better."

"You're here to check out the competition, aren't you?"

Rafael raised a finger to his lips. "Shh."

"That's sneaky," Eve said with a little smile. "I knew you had a motive for coming here."

He winked. "Just not the motive you thought."

She responded with a roll of the eyes. He noticed her long lashes fanned the high slopes of her cheeks. In the intimate light of the inn's lobby, her skin was smoother than he could have ever imagined.

Rafael was glad the tension that had built up in the car was subsiding. He wanted to make her laugh again, the way she'd laughed when they were alone in the garden. Her laughter had leaped out as if springing from a sealed cave. He'd wanted to take her in his arms and hold her close until she settled down.

"Incoming!"

Lost in the fantasy of holding her, he didn't quite understand what she was saying. "What's that?"

"Just…shut up."

She stepped up to him and brushed her lips to his in a whisper of a kiss. Rafael tensed, the muscles of his abdomen tightening. "Act like you're into it," she murmured through clenched teeth. With every nerve ending in his body setting off sparks, he didn't have to rely on dormant acting skills. He gripped her waist, pulled her close and kissed her hard, deep and slow. She gripped the lapel of his suit jacket and opened to his kiss. He heard her groan just before she tore herself away.

"I think we're good," she said, her voice shaky.

He was shaken, too. "How the hell do you figure?"

"I kissed you to create a distraction," she said. "P&J just walked in."

Paul and Jennifer Carlton were the most annoying couple in Texas, but at this moment he was making plans to send them a fruit basket and a bottle of wine.

"Here I thought you wanted to test that 'sex in an inn' theory."

"Stop thinking that," she scolded. "They're right over there. Don't look now, though."

He wouldn't dream of it. Her swollen lips had his undivided attention.

"Okay… They've entered the dining hall. You can look now."

"Nah. I'll take your word for it."

The manager returned with the keys to their suite, the one with the two distinct and separate bedrooms. The man was a little red in the face from what he'd undoubtedly witnessed.

Rafael plucked the key cards from his hand. "I'll take those. Thanks."

"Anything else, sir?"

"Send up laundry services, will you?" Rafael said. "And your best bottle of tequila."

The manager cleared his throat. "Certainly, sir. Enjoy your evening."

Don't miss what happens next in
The Rebel's Return *by Nadine Gonzalez,*
the next book in the Texas Cattleman's Club:
Fathers and Sons series!

Available February 2022 wherever
Harlequin Desire books and ebooks are sold.

Harlequin.com

HDEXP0122A

SPECIAL EXCERPT FROM

You won't want to miss
The True Cowboy of Sunset Ridge,
***the thrilling final installment of* New York Times**
bestselling author Maisey Yates's Gold Valley series!

Bull rider Colt Daniels has a wild reputation, but after losing his friend on the rodeo circuit, he's left it all behind. If only he could walk away from the temptation of Mallory Chance so easily. He can't offer her the future she deserves, but when he ends up caring for his friend's tiny baby, he needs Mallory's help. But is it temporary or their chance at a forever family?

"It's you, isn't it?"

She turned, and there he was.

So close.

Impossibly close.

And she didn't know if she could survive it.

Because those electric blue eyes were looking right into hers. But this time, it wasn't from across a crowded bar. It was right there.

Right there.

And she didn't have a deadweight clinging to her side that kept her from going where she wanted to go, doing what she wanted to do. She was free. Unencumbered, for the first time in fifteen years. For the first damn time.

She was standing there, and she was just Mallory.

Jared wasn't there. Griffin wasn't there. Her parents weren't there.

She was standing on her own, standing there with no one and nothing to tell her what to do, no one and nothing to make her feel a certain thing.

So it was all just him. Blinding electric blue, brilliant and scalding.

Perfect.

"I…I think so. Unless…unless you think I'm someone else." It was much less confident and witty than she'd intended. But she didn't feel capable of witty just now.

PHMYEXP0122

"You were here once. About six months ago."

He remembered her. He remembered her. This man who had haunted her dreams—no, not haunted, created them—who had filled her mind with erotic imagery that had never existed there before, was…talking about her. He was.

He thought of her. He remembered her.

"I was," she said.

He looked behind her, then back at her. "Where's the boyfriend?"

He asked the question with an edge of hostility. It made her shiver.

"Not here."

"Good." His lips tipped upward into a smile.

"I…" She didn't know what to say. She didn't know what to say because this shimmering feeling inside her was clearly, clearly shared and…

Suddenly her freedom felt terrifying. That freedom that had felt, only a moment before, exhilarating suddenly felt like too much. She wanted to hide. Wanted to scamper under the bar and get behind the bar stool so that she could put something between herself and this electric man. She wondered if she was ready for this.

Because there was no question what this was.

One night.

With nothing at all between them. Nothing but unfamiliar motel bedsheets. A bed she'd never sleep in again and a man she would never sleep with again.

She understood that.

PHMYEXP0122